LIES BEHIND THE WOODS

LIES BEHIND THE WOODS

BRADLEY CORNISH

Copyright

Publisher's Note:

This is a work of fiction. Names, characters, places, and incidents are a product of the author's imagination. Locales and public names are sometimes used for atmospheric purposes. Any resemblance to actual people, living or dead, or to businesses, companies, events, institutions, or locales is completely coincidental.

Follow Bradley Cornish:

www.bradleycornish.com

https://www.facebook.com/AuthorBradleyCornish

Lies Behind The Woods/Bradley Cornish. — 1st ed.

ISBN 978-0-578-59361-6

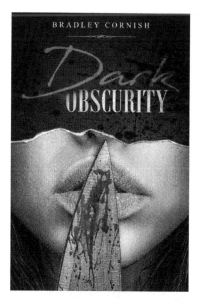

For the ones that spoke out but were never heard.

Contents

Prologue

Stockholm syndrome is a condition in which hostages develop a psychological alliance with their captors during captivity. Emotional bonds may be formed, between captor and captives, during intimate time together, but these are generally considered irrational in light of the danger or risk endured by the victims. The FBI's Hostage Barricade Database System and *Law Enforcement Bulletin* indicate that roughly 8% of victims show evidence of Stockholm syndrome. About ninety-six percent of victims involve suicide, domestic violence, and include people with previous relationships with the abuser.

This is one of those stories.

BRADLEY CORNISH

LIES
BEHIND
THE
WOODS

The Moment

As Steve approached the intersection, the tiny hairs on the back of his neck stood up. Chills ran down his spine and his heart jumped out of his chest. He froze and stood like a deer in headlights as he felt the presence of an oncoming vehicle from behind. He was surrounded by trees that made the road a picture-perfect moment of Fall in the middle of June. Suddenly, he shook as he heard the roar of the vehicle's engine ascending on him like an oncoming freight train. As a runner, he felt vulnerable and moved a little more to the left side of the road. As it got closer, the roar filled his ears. Just as he approached the crossroads at the stop sign, the pickup truck flew by—without stopping—taking the same left turn he had planned. He noticed the truck's speed was too fast to make that turn. It pitched to the right and almost rolled. Its left tires lifting off the pavement and its right tires screeching and stuttering. The truck brutally slid sideways through the junction.

Steve wanted to see the driver that was putting his life in danger, but just as he looked into the cab of the truck, he heard a woman scream thunderously from within.

He saw the driver, a peculiar man about 40ish, holding the steering wheel with his left hand, and his right arm was wrapped around the shoulders of what looked to be a young woman.

What Steve did not see, or hear, as the truck's tires squealed and chattered through the intersection, was the woman's body sliding violently across the seat as the truck made an all too fast and sharp left-hand turn. As the vehicle deviated and tilted to the right, a vigorous force attempted to tip it on its side. The woman's white shoes slammed into the side view mirror as her feet hurled through the window she had managed to open a few miles back.

The crazed driver's hand around her shoulders slipped, but he caught the joint of her elbow. If he hadn't, she would have exited the truck's window with the side view mirror that she managed to kick clean off the truck. The mirror rolled to the ground by the side of the road.

The driver gunned the truck's engine, and its tires screeched and smoked as it sped away. The smell of rubber filled his lungs. Stunned, his heart raced and his legs weakened.

Steve noticed the truck's license plate as it sped away. His internal beat told him he had just completed running two miles. "12:16 p.m.," he said to himself.

He looked around to see if anyone else had witnessed the horrendous act of reckless driving, but not another car was in sight. There was nothing around; no homes, no stores or gas stations. Simply two lonely roads crossing paths.

Steve had only gotten a brief look at the driver and an even briefer look at the young woman's face. He thought she looked to be about nineteen or twenty, but he wasn't good at guessing age.

He couldn't make out what the woman's scream was about since the pickup truck had made such a squeal of its own while sliding through the intersection. Was the young woman's scream a cry for help?

Perhaps it was the scream of a joyous thrill ride. Was the older man her father? Were the father and daughter having an argument? Was the older man her boyfriend? She looked too young for him, but this was hill country after all; who knows what they get away with up here.

Still stunned, his heart pounded as he stumbled along the road in an attempt to continue his run. He was not sure what to make of the situation. In his head, he re-played the scenarios he had just considered about the driver and the young woman. His first thought was to flag down the next car and ask to use their cell and call the police in case the woman was screaming for help. But the more he ran through those possible options, the more the odds seemed to him that the scream was in reaction to the driver's crazy driving. "A truck almost flipping in an intersection would invoke a scream from its passenger, wouldn't it?" he asked himself.

Steve's impulse for not wanting to get involved, coupled with his desire to start his vacation off on the right foot, led him to decide that the reckless driving is what warranted a scream from the young female passenger, so he decided to put it out of his mind and continue his run.

That was the event that interrupted Steve's run two miles and sixteen minutes into it. An event that would haunt him for the next three years.

Steve had been a runner ever since his high school days on the track team. Running was his escape, his tool of choice when he needed to de-stress. Brought on by traumatic events in his child-hood from his own emotional abuse. Steve just got better at running. He was a savant and had the extraordinary skill of judging when he had ran a mile, no matter what pace he was keeping or the terrain he was running on. He checked himself against his smartwatch, the iPhone, the Fitbit; he had tried them all. He kept track of the distance not by counting his strides or attempting to keep a mental clock; he kept track of his distance by the beat of his soul. He often meditated while he ran and could block out most thoughts—he did need to pay atten-tion to traffic and such for his own safety, but he could block out the noise of life. He didn't think about academics, his students, his current girlfriend and her pending expiration date, or his ailing mother. He simply ran and had a sixth sense when those soul beats in his heart added up to a mile.

And so, it was on that particular day in June. He had awoken to the first day of his summer vacation in a rental cottage in a small remote town in the Adirondack mountains. The heart and soul of White Pine. Steve always went to White Pine for his summer vacations. The same place where his father met his mother. His birthplace. A way to go back and find the missing piece of his childhood; his father, who left him years ago.

Steve woke up on this day to a warm mottled sunlight illuminating the piny woods around the cottage. It was his twenty-fifth birthday and he had spent the morning after breakfast reading. By noon, he needed a run. He tightened the laces of his running shoes on the steps of the front porch and listened to the birds. Feeling the warm breeze against his skin, he took a deep breath in. It was 12 p.m. sharp as he set out running down the quiet country road in front of the cottage. He was very familiar with the area, so he simply headed south towards the inner town. Steve was consistently averaging eight-minute miles at that time, unless he was running in really steep terrain, but the road he was on was fairly flat, with little dips and rises but nothing significant.

At 12:16 p.m., he came to that fateful intersection when his internal beat told him he had just completed two miles.

2

Hero Found

Three years later, Steve was sitting at his office desk staring out the window over the campus grounds, daydreaming about hating his job. He thought about his next run to escape the dreadful duties of grading papers. The warm sun of early May blossomed the flowerbeds; the spring semester would soon be winding down. He was between lectures, so it was the time in his schedule that he allotted to see students who were compelled to meet with him. Usually, these students were struggling and hoped a face-to-face would somehow miraculously raise their grade, but he was not one to trade favors for grades. It's not that he didn't often fantasize about bribes, it was that he valued his position too much to risk that sort of complication. Steve didn't want to mix pleasure with business. He would perform his usual psychology number on the students; he would tell them what they already knew, that they were lazy and not putting enough effort into his class. He had just sent one teary-eyed young redhead out of his office when the department administrative assistant interrupted him: "I have a young lady here. She says it's urgent she speaks with you. She is not one of your students. What should I tell her?"

Bewildered and yet intrigued, Steve said, "Send her in."

When Tara walked into Steve's office, he felt he knew her from somewhere but he couldn't place her. His mind raced through his twenty-eight-year history, but he came up blank. Before him stood an attractive young woman, he estimated all of twenty-one or twenty-two. To his eyes, she had a pleasing-looking face, not model gorgeous but cute nevertheless. Her body looked stunning and she had curves in all the right places. He thought she had a country wholesome quality about her—sexy, but ready to milk a cow if needed. Someone he would love to have fun with if given the opportunity.

Tara stood there staring at Steve. Too long a silence had fallen in the room. He wanted to break the silence and ask her what she wanted, but he froze; there was something about her that arrested him.

"Do you know who I am?" questioned the gorgeous young woman standing in front of his desk.

"No. I mean, you look familiar, but I can't place you."

"I'm Tara Murphy."

Steve's sudden paled complexion gave away the shock his brain was going through. He felt the prickled heat of guilt wash over him. Beads of perspiration formed on his face and palms. His thoughts went dry, holding him from speaking.

After another long, awkward moment of silence, he said, "Oh, yes . . . sorry . . . I wasn't expecting to ever meet you."

"I'm sorry. I should have called . . . made an appointment or something."

"No, no . . . it's fine . . . I just . . . it's been three years . . . I've tried to . . ." He wanted to say, "put it out of my mind," but he had no reason to. The tragedy was not his, it was hers. He had only been a material witness.

After yet another moment of awkward silence, he said, "So what brings you to my office today? How's your mom, by the way?"

"She's fine. She doesn't know I'm here. She is actually tied up right now. That's why I'm here," Tara said with a beautiful but mystifying smile.

Three years earlier, Steve had rented that cottage near where he grew up in the Adirondacks for the summer. Just that previous academic year, he had secured a tenured position at a liberal New York college. He worked tirelessly to pull himself up by his boot straps to the position of professor of history. Born to a poor family and raised by his divorced mother after his father abanded him, he had no easy life. As a boy, Steve and his mother lived in a small apartment in a poor part of Harlem, NY. His mother had drilled a strong work ethic in him; she didn't want to raise another bum like the brute that impregnated her. She didn't want to have to carry her son's ass all of her life. She told him over and over again, "A good education is your only way out of this hell hole. Don't disappoint me, Steven," and then she would cry. He hated to see his mother cry and would always try to console her. She worried about him falling in with a bad element, a gang or something, as she left their tiny apartment each evening to go to work as an office cleaner. But she did not need to worry. She had sufficiently laid the guilt of his father's sins on him. The father he always wanted to know. He would do anything to not burden her life any further.

Even though his mother had kicked his father out when Steve was just three years old and told him never to contact her or their son again, Steve always felt his father had abandoned him. He didn't fight to stay in the marriage, nor did he try to contact Steve after the divorce, even if his mother had forbade it. It was as if he had deliberately destroyed the marriage to unburden himself of his responsibilities. This was the story Steve's mother told him as he didn't remember these events in his life.

As a teenager, Steve often fantasized about his father. Although he blamed his father for abandoning him, he desperately wanted a normal father-son relationship with him. He thought that if his father only knew him, his father would see that he wasn't a burden, and then everything would be alright. Steve made many attempts to find his father in White Pine, but each lead led to a dead end.

Steve didn't stay in relationships long. Six months to a year and a half was his usual relationship lifespan before he would find a way to sabotage things, usually by way of cheating on his girlfriend. He tried other methods, even honesty, but being unfaithful was part of his DNA. He would find another girlfriend and then find a way to get caught in bed with her by his current one.

He had just got rid of his latest year-long love affair, but unlike his usual cheating routine, he didn't take up his typical path of relationship destruction. This time, it was his girlfriend's older sister and she was simply a nympho in his mind. He felt guilty using his girlfriend's sister like that, but at the same time, he felt free; for once not jumping from one relationship right into another. He had no doubt he could link up with another woman easily, at any time. At six feet tall, an athletic build, light brown hair, and a ruggedly charming face, he had been called "tall" and "handsome" ever since he was a teenager. This time, he was looking forward to a summer off in the mountains, free and relaxed. He had planned to read and perhaps start writing that book he promised himself he would write. Most importantly, he would look for his father.

The memory of that fateful afternoon run—the intersection, the squealing truck—flooded Steve's mind as Tara stood before him explaining that her mother was not aware she had come to visit him. "Your mother doesn't know you are here?"

"No. She doesn't need to. I'm twenty-two now, and I've been out of my mother's charge ever since I was nineteen. Since that day." Tara's eyes rolled to the ground like a sad puppy.

"Yes. I see. Where are you living then?" Steve asked, still unsure why she came to see him, but willing to make small talk. He didn't feel right cutting things that quick with her. He was sure that she must be fragile after everything she had gone through.

"I'm still in White Pine, but I'm living in town now. I've got an apartment near the movie theater," she answered.

"A job?" he inquired.

"I'm a waitress at the Pine Arms. Or at least I was. Lord knows if I'll have a job when I get back. They didn't want to give me this time off, so I told them I was leaving anyway." she shrugged.

"How long are you here for?"

"Don't know. A few days . . . maybe more."

At this point, Steve felt he had run out of small talk. "So, why did you make the five-hour journey to see me?"

Tara shrugged and then said, "To get to know you. I feel like it's my mission."

Steve grabbed the back of his neck and massaged the tension out of it as he exhaled. He then moved his hand to his face and stroked his chin as if he was stroking a goatee, even though he had no facial hair. His conscience was telling him something was off and not right, but his intrigue and Tara's beautiful physique kept him wanting to engage.

He exhaled loudly as he looked at her and pondered the situation.

Before he could speak, she said, "It's OK. I get it. You don't owe me anything. Perhaps this was a mistake."

She grabbed her handbag and turned to leave, but was interrupted by Steve's voice.

"Tara. Stop. It's fine. I'd like to get to know you too."

She turned back just before the door.

"Look . . . I just . . . I don't know what to say to you. I don't know how to act around you. I'm not good at this," he managed to stutter, reluctantly.

Tara looked Steve in the eyes and smiled again.

"How about we start from the beginning? Hi, my name is Tara, pleased to make your acquaintance."

Professor Steve suddenly felt like the student in front of this obviously mature young woman.

"Yes . . . of course. Steve here. Likewise . . . pleased," he said as he extended his hand to her.

Their handshake was more tender than he expected, and he felt a warm comfort from her hand. He pulled away first after feeling the connection had gone on too long. She smiled.

"Do you have some time? Can we get some coffee and talk?" Tara asked.

"I have a class in twenty minutes. Can we meet for lunch?"

"Yes. Of course."

"There's a quiet cafe just off campus. The Little Hen. I'll see you there at 12:20," he instructed her.

As Tara left his office, Steve couldn't stop the memories of what took place three years ago from flooding his mind. A hero, he should have never been.

3

Guilty Conscience

One week after the pickup truck had recklessly gone through that intersection two miles and sixteen minutes into Steve's first run, on his first day of his summer vacation as a sitting professor, he picked up the newspaper at the local grocery store while buying groceries. The Pine Chronicle was one of those weekly local small-town newspapers, the ones that cover cow births and missing cats. There was a section for prayer; God's Corner, and what roads were closing for construction on the message boards. The paper was filled with lots of used-car ads and items for sale. It wasn't the kind of paper he usually read and he couldn't even remember what possessed him to add it to his cart amongst the steak, broccoli, beer, and ice cream. If pressed, he might have said he was looking for a hint of local entertainment. Someplace he might find female companionship. He hadn't spent a week alone in quite a while, and he was already getting tired of the fantasy—he was hungry for the real thing.

During dinner, he grabbed the paper and flipped through it. He saw a few ads for pubs and thought he might make his way to one later that night to see what kind of local action there might be in White Pine. He was just about to toss the paper onto the heap of newspapers next to the wood stove when he noticed the back page.

In large print were the words: **MISSING PERSON**.

Normally, he wouldn't have given much thought about a missing person in an area where he was only vacationing, but there was a picture of a young woman under those big letters. That face of the young woman looked familiar to him for some reason, so he read the article.

"**HAVE YOU SEEN HER?**" the brief article asked the readership. "If so, call the police on this number…" The article went on to say that the police were looking for a missing teen from White Pine. No foul play was suspected at this time, and they were not releasing her name due to the nature of privacy requested by the family. The police were still investigating, and it was too early to give any more details. Steve thought it was strange that the paper would print a picture of the girl's face, but no name. Surely, in this small town, many people would know who she was.

Maybe they were afraid that some nut-job would prey on her family's grief if her name got out. Some nut-job from far away because, surely, many residents in the town must know the family, the whole town being of only about one thousand permanent residents, not counting the weekenders or the summer tourists.

The more he looked at the picture, the more he remembered the events of his run a week ago: the speeding truck and crazy-looking driver holding onto a young woman with one hand while driving with the other. A knot formed in his stomach. He suddenly felt flush with guilt. One thought gripped his mind: "Was the girl in that truck this same young girl pictured in the paper?"

One other thought flooded his mind: "I may have witnessed an abduction."

He suddenly felt that he should have done something right away, a week ago right after that incident during his run. He chastised himself; he should have flagged down the next vehicle and told them about the apparent abduction, and asked—no, demanded—to use their phone to call the police. But then again, maybe this wasn't the same girl. Maybe he was jumping to conclusions, again.

He decided not to go out that night looking to get laid. His mind kept going back to that incident in the intersection the week before. He retired to bed early instead, but he had a terrible night's sleep.

He kept waking up and asking himself, "what if the paper girl is the truck girl? What if there's still hope? What if she is still alive?" He vowed to go to the police the very next morning.

When Steve arrived at the Little Hen, Tara was already there. She was sitting at a table and motioned to him as he walked through the door.

"So, you've come all this way just to get to know me?" Steve asked as he settled into his chair.

Tara looked at him coldly without answering. By her expression, he guessed that his patronizing tone had cut her.

"Can I ask what you hope to get out of this? Some sort of closure, perhaps?"

He felt out of place and unsettled. He had learned

to deal with the guilt he had over his delay in going to the police, but her sudden appearance

brought everything back to life again. "Look . . . you said earlier you were OK with this.

If you don't want to do this, I can leave," she answered abruptly while removing her napkin from her lap and throwing it on the placemat in front of her.

"OK. You're right. I'm sorry. This is all still new to me," he explained.

"Why are you the one who has issues with this? I went through the ordeal, not you," Tara demanded.

"I still feel guilty. OK? If I had acted earlier, you wouldn't have had to endure all that . . ." his voice trailed off. "That" was the thing he couldn't bear to think about; what had happened to her during the week he delayed going to the police. "Maybe they could have found you that same day and . . . and everything would have been different."

"But you did act, and it saved my life! OK, maybe it was late, but I'm alive now. If you hadn't come forward, I wouldn't be here today. If you hadn't shown up, life would be different for you and I. He definitely would have killed me sooner or later."

"How can you be so level-headed about this? How are you not messed up?" Steve asked.

"I don't know. I should be messed up, you're right. That's where most people in my position would have ended up. But you know what? I didn't want to be all fucked-up. Sure, I had my fucked-up time after the police rescued me, but I made a decision. Not right away, but I decided that the incident was not going to define me. I wasn't going to let some nut-job ruin my life."

"I applaud you for being so mature about it. I don't know if I could handle that if I was in your shoes. So, I suppose you have forgiven that bastard for what he did to you?" Steve said while looking at the menu.

"No. Of course not. That's bullshit. I'll never forgive that cold-hearted motherfucker. I'll always hate him. But this is not about him. It's about me not being the victim. I've moved on. There's nothing to gain from repeating the past over and over again and saying "poor me". I need to be better, do better, and move on."

At this point, the waitress came to the table and took their orders.

As Steve began to relax, he realized he was the one projecting what he had felt about the incident onto Tara. The more she spoke, the more he admired her maturity, her sense of self-assurance; those qualities were now attractive to him. As they sat talking across the table from each other in The Little Hen, he started admiring her features: her blue eyes; her auburn hair; a freckle or two left over from puberty; her ample bosom and her exposed cleavage, that he only now allowed himself to notice.

Her Victoria's Secret scent had Steve wanting to lean closer to her body. Had she selected that blouse to arouse him? In light of the evidence of her maturity, and her ease with her past traumatic event, he now thought maybe she had dressed to impress him. He caught himself staring at her breasts and then reprimanded himself. He was confused. He didn't know how he should treat her. The six-year age difference didn't bother Steve at all, but he couldn't help but view Tara as a younger sister, or as someone whose life he once saved.

"I want to know everything about you," Tara said to him with a smile that reminded Steve of her mother.

During lunch, Steve and Tara shared some of their fondest childhood memories.

At a silence in the conversation, Steve's curiosity got the best of him and he asked, "So, how are you really doing, Tara? I mean, with everything that happened three years ago."

"As I told you, I'm not going to be the victim here. I've come to terms with the fact that I did nothing to deserve what happened. That some random sick-o, scum of the earth dirtbag, picked on me out of the blue, that's all." A sullen look washed over her face as her gaze fell to the plate in front of her.

"Did he . . ." he started.

"What do you want to know, Steve? Exactly what he did to me . . . every detail?" Her tone suddenly had some bite to it as she stared directly into his eyes.

"I'm sorry . . . it's none of my business," he tried to recover, a little embarrassed that he'd asked.

"Well, if it's anyone's business, I suppose it's yours. You were a part of that, Steve, whether you wanted to be or not." Her tone softened again. She looked at him with attentive eyes.

"Let's just say, he didn't strip me naked and tie me to his bed so he could just look at me, Steve. He didn't abduct me because he needed a chess partner." Her eye's reddened and her lips pursed. "It was two weeks of hell . . ." she stopped.

He looked at her with sullen eyes, crestfallen. "I don't have the words to express how sorry I am. I should have . . ."

"What's done is done," she interrupted him. "We can't go back and undo what happened. I've moved forward. You need to as well. We both need to."

They sat in silence looking at one another sadly. When the silence was no longer bearable, they changed the subject and resumed small talk as they finished their lunch.

"I've got nowhere to stay tonight. Can I stay with you?" Tara suddenly blurted out as the check for their lunch came.

Steve was taken aback. He hadn't anticipated this. On one hand, his guilty conscience thought it was the least he could do as a good gesture after her travels. On the other hand, Steve felt out of place and thought this was an odd request in a short time. He had a spare bedroom, but he didn't feel comfortable with her sleeping in his apartment. He didn't know her that well and he didn't trust himself with her.

But what kind of a jerk would he come off as if he said she couldn't crash at his place? This is what he thought as he reluctantly said, "Sure . . . I have a spare room. You can stay the night."

Later that day, inside the kitchen of his apartment, Tara moved close to Steve. She backed him up against the kitchen counter. Her breasts pressed against his chest. She moved her hand to his crotch and started massaging him there as she looked up into his eyes. "I want to make you happy," she said in a sultry voice.

Steve felt instantly conflicted. In almost any other circumstance, he would have loved having a beautiful young woman of Tara's charms come on to him, but the past seized his mind and blocked him.

"No. No. This isn't right," Steve said as he slid to the side and out from under her clutch.

"Why not?" Tara questioned. "We're both adults. I've been thinking of this for the past year; it's all I can think of. I want to thank you for saving my life."

"That's where the problem begins, Tara. Let's put aside that I've had sex with your mother for a moment. The real issue here is that I saved your life. This puts our relationship dynamics on an uneven footing right from the start. There may even be some exploitation going on here. One could easily say that I would be taking advantage of you."

"Do you always feel as if you're taking advantage of a woman when you make love to her?" she asked.

It was a logical and reasonable question considering what he had just said. Steve's desire for not staying with a woman for more than a year and a half ran through his daddy-issue mind. He didn't think he had ever taken advantage of his girlfriends when they made love as it was mutual lovemaking. And he did happen to fall in love with some of his short-term lovers. He just couldn't stay the course and didn't know why. He had never really analyzed what made him sabotage every single relationship. Steve just loved having multiple relationships.

Steve was digging deep into his flawed character in an attempt to resist Tara. Her cleavage mesmerized him as the tops of her exposed breasts rose and fell while she breathed. He wanted nothing more than to dive into those wholesome country-bred mounds—to tear away her blouse and expose her milky white bosom. His testosterone couldn't hold him back as he wanted to see what her nipples looked like; he imagined they were large and pointy, with rosy but pimply arreolas. He could easily imagine sliding his big hard erection between her ample breasts. Those were the thoughts he was trying desperately to keep at bay.

"I can't," he said, moving away from her. He was trying to do the right thing this time.

He was still carrying a heavy load for not going to the police right away. If only I had, he thought.

What Tara had endured during those two weeks when she was held captive was never spoken of; not by the police; not by the paper, the Pine Chronicle; not by the pretty young DA who Steve had a sexual encounter with; and least of all, not by Tara's mother, who threw herself at Steve in an attempt to thank him for saving her daughter's life. Perhaps that was it: he had already had thank-you sex. Perhaps he felt he would be betraying her mother by getting a thank-you orgasm from her daughter also. Not that he had kept in contact with Tara's mother over these past few years, but still, what would she think? What kind of animal would she think he was if she found out that he had sex with Tara too?

Tara moved closer to Steve again, trapping him once more against the counter. She slowly slid her hand up his thigh and back to his crotch. She could tell he was interrested; his erection betrayed his words.

They looked into each other's eyes for a long moment. She tilted her head to him. He almost lowered his face to hers for a kiss, but then caught himself. He gently removed her hand from his crotch. He was trying to do the right thing, whatever that was. He had never done the right thing before, not with any of his ex-girlfriends, and not about manning up and going to the police right away three years ago. He was making amends for past sins—both his and his father's.

"I'm tired. I'll see you in the morning. Everything you need is in the spare bedroom. There are extra pillows and another blanket in the closet. The hall bath is yours; I have a bathroom in my room."

Tara gave Steve a teasing look for not coming on to her, or more precisely, for not allowing her to come on to him. As Steve lay in bed that night, he couldn't help but replay the incident in his head. He mulled over the details he had later learned about how a camera had come to be placed in that intersection. How he was not really the hero but the flying mirror was. It was killing his guilty conscience.

4

The Flying Mirror

A year before Steve had witnessed the abduction, the University of White Pine secured a grant to develop a new type of intelligent traffic-enforcement camera. The camera would record a constant stream of video, which would be analyzed by a super computer at the university. The computer software would direct the operations of a second camera and be the first traffic camera for surveillance in the city.

Future presidential candidate and state senator, Alan Smith, beamed as he was interviewed by the Pine Chronicle editor in chief—who was actually the only editor and only reporter on staff—about the grant and just how significant it was to the University of White

Pine and the students enrolled in both the computer science and the electrical engineering curriculum.

"The state is looking for the students to use artificial intelligence to guide the operations of the camera," said the senator. "The software should be developed to detect if something looks suspicious about an automobile, or anyone within the automobile. Especially any illegal hunting within city limits. If the vehicle passing under the camera's field of view looks suspicious, then the camera should zoom in and take more pictures with increasing levels of detail for the police to possibly use in case the vehicle was later suspected in a crime. If the suspicious activity was serious enough, the camera would need to alert the police immediately. This is a great day for Pine County. The first of its kind in the state."

The Pine Chronicle article went on to cite that there were similar intelligent camera systems in place in big cities, but that they were linked to a much bigger system and tied to super computers. This intelligent camera would be developed strictly for rural areas with rural budgets, and the suspicious activities would be tailored to rural activities; for example, game poaching might be something an upstate rural community would be interested in, whereas a bigger city would have little need to monitor for that.

University of White Pine professor, Tim Pembleton, would lead the project. Professor Pembleton wasted no time setting up a special course for the state-funded project. Only the professor and his brightest students would work on it. This was going to be a breakout moment for his career; nothing this big, or small, had ever come his way before. He named the project the Pembleton Camera.

By the end of the year, and just before the summer that Steve had rented the cottage in White Pine, it was obvious that the development of the camera system was going slower than anyone had anticipated. Professor Pembleton had set up a rare summer program to extend the work throughout the summer break.

He asked his students to continue with the work via the summer program, and most were eager to oblige. This special summer session would begin the second week in June.

A few weeks into the summer session, the students had a working prototype. It didn't do much in the way of artificial intelligence detection, but they had managed to program a basic algorithm and were anxious to try it out in a real-world setting. The campus parking lot was not very busy during the summer, so they needed to set it up on an actual road. The students decided an intersection in White Pine would be ideal. The pattern-matching software would learn what the normal traffic would look like for the site, and any sort of anomaly would be signaled.

The camera would then zoom in and snap a lot of pictures. It was a start. The camera, in its final form, was planned to be a stand-alone smart camera. Each camera would contain all its own intelligence with a recording process and would upload non-priority data to a central server asynchronously as the server asked for it. Only when the camera detected a potential crime would the camera alert the central server and anyone monitoring for those alerts, and send data in real-time. The students hadn't yet programmed in any remote-control access for monitoring or maintaining the camera itself; the students responsible for that weren't part of the summer program.

After many vigorous days working on the final camera design, a prototype had been completed. This first Pembleton prototype could only record and analyze images and then manipulate the high-resolution camera. Any images and alerts it would have sent to a server, for now, would be stored in the camera's memory for the students to later analyze. It was a start, and they were anxious to see if the algorithm software worked in a real-world setting.

Pembleton didn't bother to get the Department of Transportation involved with the placement of the camera. After all, it would only be up for a few days, a week at the most. It would take all summer for the Department of Transportation to finish just the plan for mounting the camera. So, Pemblton and three students had thrown a ladder on a borrowed pickup truck and mounted the camera themselves. Pemblton picked an intersection that he himself drove through on his way to the college campus every morning. He figured he could keep an eye on it that way during his commute to and from work, and if he wanted to, he could perform some unusual and suspicious-looking driving acts while going through the intersection to see if the camera would pick them up.

When Steve arrived at the local police station one week into that unfortunate summer vacation day, his palms were sweaty, as though he had performed a crime himself. In hindsight, and in light of the missing persons article in the Pine Chronicle, he was certain his initial instinct was correct. He was racked with guilt over not following his gut and calling the police right away when he witnessed the reckless pickup truck allegedly abducting a young woman. All the other scenarios he had replayed in his mind that day now seemed like a pure burden. Those other scenarios he had repeated—the disciplining father, the older boyfriend out for a joy ride with his teenage soon-to-be bride—enabled him to not get involved and carry on with his vacation. His yearly mission to find his father. He felt guilty when he thought of his selfishness.

"What can we do for you?" asked the desk officer on duty.

Steve presented the last page of the Pine Chronicle. "I might have witnessed something to do with this," he said nervously.

Until then, the White Pine Police Department had no leads in the case of young Tara Murphy. Only her mother's report that she never returned from her daily walk. The police were reluctant to even call it a missing persons event at first, believing that the young girl was probably having the time of her life staying with friends or relatives. She and her mother'd had a disagreement that very same day. In her mother's report, she stated that it wasn't much of a disagreement, and that her daughter would never not come home without permission, but the police know that family members always underestimate the severity of a disagreement and always believe that their children are angels.

"What exactly did you witness?" the desk officer asked.

"A truck with a screaming girl. It almost ran me over in an intersection. A week ago. Her feet were hanging out the window."

"Sarge!" the desk officer yelled to the office behind him. The police station was small enough that there was no need to use phones or an intercom device.

The sergeant appeared from his office a moment later. "What's up?" Sarge asked his deputy at the desk. "This man has something to report on that missing girl case."

"You don't say? Well, come on back here, sir. We'll talk in my office." Sergeant Timothy Case motioned to Steve.

Steve proceeded to tell Sergeant Tim about the events he had witnessed in the intersection one week ago, two miles and sixteen minutes into his run. He told the cop about the out-of-control pickup truck, and the screaming girl being held tightly by the crazy driver. Her white shoes hanging out the window of the truck. And that he thought—no, upon reflection, he was almost certain—the same girl that was pictured in the paper was the one who screamed in that truck, but he couldn't make out a word of the scream.

When he was asked how he knew what time of day

he was in the intersection, he went on to tell the sergeant about his well-honed internal running clock; that he could pace off a mile anywhere, anytime, and how he has checked his internal clock against Apple watches, Fitbits, and the like. He told them he set off running at 12 p.m. sharp, and his internal running clock ticked off two miles at the intersection, and he was on an eight-minute-mile pace.

"Why didn't you report this earlier?" the officer asked in a judgmental tone.

"I wasn't sure. At the time, I thought it might have been a father-daughter argument, or just some people out for a joyride.

It wasn't until I saw the missing persons article in the Pine Chronicle that I . . ."

"Well, I'm glad you came forward. Until now, we hadn't a clue what happened to her," Sarge interrupted him. "Did you happen to get the license plate number?"

"I did see the license plate, and I thought I made a mental note of it, but I can't remember one number of it now for the life of me. I was awake all night last night trying to remember all the details. The plate number, it's just gone from my memory," Steve said, now feeling even more guilty, and useless.

"The truck was a dark color. Either green or blue or

something like that. I've never been good at identifying vehicles by make or model."

The Sergeant interviewed Steve for an hour, getting all the details he could out of the human pedometer. When he was through, he gave Steve his personal cell number and told him to call him anytime, day or night, if he remembered anything else, especially any of the license plate numbers.

The sergeant escorted Steve out of the police station. In the parking lot, he said, "I really thought that we had a case of a teenage runaway here. Thanks for coming forward on this. Even if it's been a week, there still might be hope. I'll be taking charge of this case myself, so you call me if you remember anything else. Anything, OK? You are doing a good thing, young man."

"Yes, I certainly will," Steve acknowledged. "Hmm . . . I wonder where she is," Sarge said as he stared off into the distance. A few moments later, his focus came back to the present and he said, "Well, I'm headed over to process the crime scene right now. Remember, call me if you can remember anything else—big or small."

During the drive from the police station back to his rental cottage, Steve felt sick. He had a knot in the pit in his stomach. His mind kept bouncing between his guilt and worry for the woman he saw in the cab of the truck.

When Sergeant Tim arrived at the scene, Professor Pembleton was up on his ladder retrieving the first prototype of the Pembleton Camera. What Professor Pembleton hadn't known, yet, was when he put the camera up on the utility pole eight days earlier, in his haste to mount the camera before anyone from the Department Of Transportation saw him, he forgot to tighten the mounting bolt securely. That very same day, not an hour after he had mounted the camera, a red-tailed hawk landed on the camera. To the hawk, it looked like an inviting place to hunt for small prey along the road. When the hawk landed on the camera, it shifted the camera out of position. The camera was no longer aiming at the center of the intersection. It wasn't aiming within the intersection at all. It was aiming straight down at the dirt off to the side of the road. The shoulder of the road was the focus of the Pembleton Camera.

"What have you got up there?" Sarge yelled up to Pembleton. Busted, Pembleton climbed down and explained the project. To give him and the project weight, and in an attempt to deflect any police inter-ference, he explained how it was state-funded through a grant, and how Senator Alan Smith himself was sponsoring it and was looking for results soon. What Pembleton didn't know, yet, was that there had been a crime at that very intersection, and Pembleton's camera was now state evidence. Much to Pembleton's objection, Sarge confiscated the camera. Pembleton tried, in vain, to maintain control of the device. He told the sergeant he would work with the police and get them all the information the camera had recorded, and that only he and his students knew how to retrieve the information off the device. The sergeant wasn't having any of it. He was confident the state's digital forensics team could handle whatever was inside that thing.

After confiscating the camera and sending Pembleton on his way, Sarge proceeded to close down the intersection and examine the crime scene. The skid marks from the squealing truck's tires were still visible, so he took pictures and measured them. He was convinced this was the crime scene Steve detailed in his report, and he knew he didn't have all the skills necessary to process it, so he sent for a special State Police crime scene investigation team to process the scene. After all, a girl's life was at stake; she may still be alive. Now that he had evidence of an abduction, he also put out the necessary alerts and bulletins and other procedural matters involved with a case like this. After all, it was his town and it could be a big career move to solve this case.

What the crime scene investigative team found from analyzing the camera was that the only thing that matched an odd pattern and came into the camera's field of view, was the truck's mirror that Tara managed to kick off the truck, which rolled into view and rested upside down. The artificial intelligence software had worked, in as much as it recognized that the mirror bolting into its view, seemingly from out of nowhere, was an anomaly. It was an odd event for what the camera had learned to be a rather boring existence aiming just off the shoulder of the road. The camera performed admirably. It zoomed in and snapped a dozen pictures of the mirror, in ever-increasing detail. The last picture the camera took clearly showed the part number of the mirror stamped onto the bottom of it.

"That's funny. I didn't find a mirror at the crime scene," Sergeant Tim mentioned to the investigative team lead as they were briefing him.

"Oh, yes . . . there's one more thing," the crime scene investigative team lead mentioned. "Almost twenty-four hours after the mirror came into the camera's view, a hand was seen retrieving the mirror from the side of the road. We didn't get anything else on the hand, or who it belonged to." It turns out a local scrap collector saw the mirror and picked it up, thinking he may be able to sell it to someone for a few bucks.

S teve fell asleep remembering the details of the incident. He awoke when he heard his bedroom door open and felt the presence of someone in his room.

"Tara?"

She slipped into bed next to him. "No, Tara. I thought we settled this."

"I can't sleep alone. I just want to lie next to you. I won't touch you. Please?"

He didn't speak. His sigh was enough for Tara to stay. True to her word, she didn't touch him that night, at least not his crotch.

Tara fell asleep quickly by his side. She had turned on her right side with her back to him and her butt snuggled up to his hip. It had been about a year since Steve had a female sleep next to him. His appetite for women had diminished, and a year ago, he just stopped wanting to date anyone. His self-condemnation over his delay in going to the police, and what he imagined

Tara had gone through that week, haunted him. It ate at his self-esteem and dulled his libido. Tara's warm body now resting next to him revived some of his old, raunchy feelings. He felt his lust building, but he was fully conscious of who was lying next to him and his desire to not take advantage of her. Steve knew something was off with Tara, but he just couldn't put his finger on it.

With Tara sleeping next to him, he couldn't help but think about the incident; with his lust building, he couldn't help but think of the pretty DA assigned to Tara's case. Steve fell asleep dreaming of Jane . . .

5

DA Jane Goodwright

A week or so after the police rescued Tara from what some said was certain death, Steve was awoken by a knock on his rental cottage door. He stumbled out of bed naked with his usual morning erection. In the middle of his half-sleep, he went out of the bedroom and into the main cottage living room. He saw someone standing at the door through the large glass window of the door. There was no curtain on the window. Once he realized he was naked and in plain view of whoever was at the door, he went into the bathroom to grab a towel.

With a tented towel wrapped around his waist, Steve answered the door.

"Hi. What . . . ah . . . it's early . . . who the hell are

you? Sorry . . . I'm still half asleep . . . what can I do for you?"

"Hello. Sorry to bother you so early. My name is Jane Goodwright. I'm the assistant DA in charge of the Tara Murphy case," she said as she showed him her court badge.

"Tara who?" Steve was confused. He had never heard the woman's name before. The police were careful not to use her name when they talked to Steve. The paper was also advised not to print her name.

"Tara Murphy. The missing girl case you helped the police crack. I'm prosecuting John Dexter, the man who abducted her."

Steve had heard the name John Dexter. His name was printed by the paper in the article about the ex-convict who abducted a local girl and kept her captive in his rented cabin deep within the woods. The paper refrained from printing any details about what he did to her during the time he had held her captive, but nonetheless, they made certain everyone knew this John Dexter was an ex-con from down state. He was the piece of shit the paper kept talking about.

"Oh . . . yes . . . come . . . come on in," he said, groggy from sleep and unaware he still had an erection tenting his towel. "Make yourself comfortable," he motioned to the couch as he went into the bedroom to put on some clothes.

When he came back into the living room, he sat on the opposite side of the couch, facing Jane.

"I need some details on what you saw in that intersection. Tell me everything you know."

"I already gave the police a full report. There's nothing more to say."

"I've read the report, but I need to hear it from you. Police reports may not be accurate. My job is to prosecute this man. I don't want him to get off on a technicality."

Steve repeated everything he had told Sergeant Tim a few weeks earlier.

And Jane repeated the same judgmental question Sergeant Tim asked, "Why did you wait for a week before going to the police?"

Steve, looking down at the floor in shame, repeated the various scenarios he had repeated in his head that led him to conclude the girl's scream was in reaction to some sort of joyride, and that he should just mind his own business.

"I think I have everything I need from you today. Stay in town. I might need to ask you some more questions," Jane ordered him as she stood up and walked to the cottage's front door. She turned around and looked at him as he stood and came to see her out. Although her face was expressionless, he thought he detected a smile in her eyes before she turned and left without another word.

A week later, Steve was sitting at the bar in the Pine Arms, a local pub and eatery that he started to frequent in hopes of finding some female companionship. Now that the missing girl was rescued, he felt once again like going out on the prowl.

As he sat drinking his beer, Jane Goodwright walked in. She noticed an empty bar stool next to him and asked, "Is this seat taken?"

"It's all yours," he replied and gestured with his hand for her to sit.

"Hi, Steve. How have you been?" Jane asked with the same inquiring voice she questioned him with a week ago.

"Fine. And you?"

"Busy with the case, but otherwise doing well." Jane ordered a gin and tonic.

"Are we supposed to be talking? I mean . . . like this . . . not officially, but socially? Isn't there a word for that? Ex-parte or something?" Steve asked.

"No. Ex-parte would be, for example, if I learned some of the facts in your eyewitness testimony were fabricated, and I went to the judge with that information without notifying the defense council. It doesn't apply here. Besides, you're the state's witness, not defense. I would have no reason to go to the judge, as in that example. At most, the two of us fraternizing would be an ethical issue for me," Jane explained.

"Oh . . . well, aren't you worried about being un-ethical?"

"It's not that big a deal. The case is all but wrapped up. The police caught him red-handed. He's trying to plead insanity, but it makes little difference. Since he didn't kill her, there's no death penalty on the table. The evidence is overwhelmingly stacked against him, so he's going away for a long time, insane or not. The insanity plea is just stalling. Besides, we have enough witnesses to his sanity. No jury is going to free him and the public defender assigned to his case hates the creep, so it will never go to trial. She'll convince him to take a plea. They may knock a few years off and offer him a chance for parole, but he'll be such an old man by the time he serves the mandatory sentence that he won't be able to get it up to kidnap anyone again. That's if he survives prison. The other inmates don't take kindly to woman-predators behind bars."

"Well, in that case, drink up," Steve said as he downed the last of his beer and flagged the bartender down for another round for Jane and him.

"So, what brings a pretty woman like you to White Pine?" he asked.

"How do you know I'm not from around here?" Jane played along.

"Oh, just a hunch. You seem to dress a little more urban than the average White Piner."

"If I had been born here, I might take offense to that," she said with a slim smile.

"A-ah . . . so I was right then. Your shoes are a dead giveaway. You see, a woman born in the mountains, no matter how much education she obtains or how much she aspires to dress like her city counter-part, will always choose sturdy shoes. Not necessarily hiking boots for every occasion, but the sturdiest of the soles within the style category they're shopping for," he postulated in a half-joking tone.

Jane looked down at her heels. She tilted her head slightly and widened her eyes and pursed her lips. "Well, you got me there. It seems I do have the thinnest heels around these parts.

"I moved here six months ago after a divorce. I was assistant DA down state in a suburb of New York City, Tarrytown. Next to the famous Sleepy Hollow.

Not too exciting really. My ex-husband has a law firm there and he was certainly not going to move, so I decided I had to. That town is too small for the both of us—divorced, that is. Too many shared friends and lovers. Don't ask me why I chose White Pine, I don't know. They had an opening for a DA and I needed to get out of Tarrytown."

"You sound as if you regret moving here," Steve responded curiously.

"Oh, I don't know, it's a charming little place all right, and everyone has been real nice. The dating pool seems a little thin, that's all.

"In fact, I haven't dated anyone since I moved here," Jane said as she looked Steve up and down. She slowly crossed and then uncrossed her legs. She put her elbow on the bar, brought her right hand to her chin, and tilted her head, slightly resting it on her hand. She tapped the corner of her lip with her pinky finger as her lips played out a self-amused smile.

Steve felt as if he had just been mind-fucked, and the response between his legs confirmed that he liked it. He fidgeted on his bar stool in an attempt to adjust his pants for more room in his crotch. Jane noticed this and her smile widened.

Three drinks had gone down easily while they conversed about all manner of topics. There was a lot of laughter, some light touching to make a point, and the occasional foot caress of the other's leg, not to mention the all-out flirting. By the time those three drinks settled in their bellies, you could cut the sexual tension in the air with a knife. Jane signaled first. She tilted her head towards the door and said, "Wanna get out of here?"

Steve wasted no time paying the bill. When they were outside the Pine Arms, they fell into each other's arms. The kiss was as passionate as if they had been long-lost lovers finally reunited.

"Follow me. I'm just three miles from here," Jane directed Steve in a sexy voice as she opened her car door.

Once inside her house, Steve pawed at Jane's blouse and she at his pants button. They put in all they could do to keep from ripping each other's clothes off. Jane stepped back and pulled her blouse over her head. She then removed her bra. Steve saw Jane's big breasts and perky hard nipples staring at him. They were not too large, but rather, they were naturally perfect. Steve stood there for a moment and took in the sight of topless Jane. As a breast man, he relished the moment when a new lover exposed her breasts to him for the first time. His mother breastfed him until the age of five as a way of compensating for her broken marriage, and he credited that for his fascination with female breasts. He admired all shapes and sizes, and always evaluated how they would look bra-less in a sheer white blouse. It was a little thought exercise he would always indulge in. He was pleased that Jane could easily have gotten away without a bra for support, that is. You would know she had breasts if she wore a blouse with no bra. He liked that her nipples weren't the type to protrude out like small round tubes. She had large pink areolas that blended seamlessly into puffy cone-shaped nipples. Steve grabbed them. Squeezed them. Then started to suck on them as Jane rubbed his head and let out a slight moan.

He moved back into her arms. They lip-locked again for a long deep kiss, their tongues picking up where they left off from the parking lot of the Pine Arms, dancing that age-old lust tango, and getting to know one another—tastebud to tastebud. As they kissed, Steve's hands moved back to her perky breasts and his fingers massaged her nipples. Eager to massage those luscious cones with his tongue again, he broke from their mouth dance and moved his lips to her right breast. At first, a tender love bite, and then he sucked her entire nipple into his mouth and covered it with his tongue.

Jane squealed with passion as he nibbled and massaged her breasts, first one then the other.

"Ooow . . . I love having my nipples devoured like that. That's it . . . bite them . . . suck 'em hard. Aaah . .

. yes, like that . . . ohhh . . . sparks . . . right to my body, baby," she moaned as she tilted her head back.

Steve watched as Jane reached under her skirt and started playing with herself as he continued to administer his attention to her smooth body.

After a few moments, she pushed his head away from her breasts. "Get naked and make yourself comfortable. I need to freshen up a bit," she said as she skipped to the bathroom.

Steve removed his clothes and found her bed. He pulled back her bed linens and jumped in with his erection pointing to the ceiling. He gently stroked himself as he waited for her to finish freshening up.

Jane soon appeared in her bedroom doorway, naked, and looking even more confident than she had appeared earlier that evening. She smiled as she saw Steve naked, making eye contact with her.

Her left index finger went to the corner of her mouth and she bit the tip of her finger, while her right hand drifted to her bush and her fingers found her inner-self and massaged it.

Steve saw her in the doorway. He smiled at her as he continued to massage himself. Jane watched him lustfully. After a few moments, she strode across the room, climbed onto her bed and slithered up to Steve's toned body.

She lowered her face to his shaft and whispered, "Umm . . . where have I seen this big boy before?"

"Your pleasure is at his command," Steve playfully added as he stopped stroking himself and awaited her command.

"Oh, don't stop stroking it. I love to watch a man play with his own joystick. It's a real turn-on for me."

Steve obliged and returned his hand to his erection. Jane reached for her own body and teased herself. With her face just an inch from Steve, she breathed heavily on his shaft as she moaned in ecstasy bringing herself to the brink of culmination.

She stuck out her tongue and moved in to taste Steve. She let out a sweet sound as she licked up his shaft to the tip of his erection, then licked around his mushroom head as if it were an ice cream cone in need of a lick before the ice cream melted and dripped down the side of the cone.

Steve let out audible tones of pleasure as Jane's tongue explored every nook and cranny of him. She finally gave him mercy and stuffed his entire erection into her mouth. She swallowed him deeply and proceeded to pleasure him as his muscle pulsed and danced.

Jane took her time playing with Steve and rubbing his muscles with a light touch. She would stop often and let his body pulse and dance in her bed. She would attack again, making him feel relaxed and aroused. Her foreplay took several minutes as she admired Steve. Her tongue circled around his rock-hard abs, pressing her body against his. She nibbled at it like she was eating an ear of corn, sucking and tenderly biting him. She repeated this series of moves again and again, each time stopping at the lips to savor her reward, his tongue dancing with hers.

Steve had never been loved with so much passion and enthusiasm. She repeated her sex-crazed worship. Devouring him as if she were a starving woman finally allowed to eat.

Jane gave him one final kiss before she crawled down his body and straddled it, ready to ride the mechanical bull named Steve.

Her turn now, Steve flipped her body to position himself on top. He looked deeply into her eyes in admiration. Steve inhaled her sweet smell, and this only made him want to please her more. But when he attempted to drive his tongue down and between her legs, she pulled up, teasing him.

He grabbed her hips in an attempt to position her higher so his tongue could get at the object of his desire, but she would have none of it. She held her ground, just tempting his lust more.

She taunted him for another minute, and then said, "Enough of this teasing. I want you now," she howled, as she positioned herself to his eager mouth.

He drove his tongue into her waiting and lathered the space between her thighs. He couldn't get his tongue in deep enough as she swirled and grinded herself on his face. She moaned and clamped her thighs around his head as she rode his face like a jockey taking a race horse to the finish.

Soon, she repositioned herself so only her labia was above his wanting lips. Steve grabbed her thighs and pulled her in tighter to his face. Jane begged Steve not to stop as she closed her eyes and exhaled slowly. His tongue and her pool of moisture joined together until he wrestled a powerful orgasm from deep within her groin.

Steve slowly kissed her body as he moved up to her lips. They kissed passionately for what seemed like an eternity.

Steve felt that old familiar feeling, the magic he felt whenever he first penetrated a new lover and his hard body felt her for the first time. He thrust his hips upward in an attempt to reach deeper into her body. Jane reached her hands to his hips and held him tight, a signal to him not to let go. He surrendered to her gesture and melted away with love.

They tangled like newlyweds on a honeymoon night. Slowly at first, then faster and faster until sweat ran across their bodies and they both exploded together in one big orgasmic climax.

Awakening in the middle of the night from his dream of Jane, with his hard-on pulsing against the sheets and Tara lying next to him sleeping, he was brought back to his present circumstances. Namely, that he wouldn't allow himself to use that hard-on on Tara. Frustrated, he rolled over and fell back asleep.

When he awoke the next morning, Tara was snuggling up against him, her head on his chest and her arm draped over his waist.

"Good morning," she said as Steve came to life and focused on the situation. "You're a quiet sleeper. I didn't even hear one snore from you last night," she added, smiling.

Steve felt the remnants of last night's erotic dream of Jane, his morning erection. He was still trying to be good and not seduce Tara, but his libido was fighting the logical side of his mind. He knew he had to get out of bed before his erection won out. He moved her arm off his waist and slid out of bed, keeping his back to her. Steve always slept naked. He attempted to conceal his erection with his pillow, but in his half-awake state, he forgot his backside was bare, so he exposed his buttocks to her as he headed to his bathroom.

"Nice buns," Tara let out.

"This isn't going to be easy," he said under his breath as he slipped into the bathroom. It was a Saturday. There would be no classes that day for Steve to escape to. He would have Tara with him all day. He took a cold shower to knock down his lust-filled erection. When he came back to his bedroom with a towel wrapped around his waist,

Tara was not in bed where he had left her. He dressed, and as he walked down the hall towards the kitchen, he smelled breakfast cooking.

"I hope you're hungry. I'm making bacon and eggs," she said as she looked over her shoulder at him as he entered the kitchen.

"Starved," he replied. He sat down at the table and she brought a cup of coffee to him. It was then he noticed she was still dressed in her nightgown under a man's plain white shirt—the shirt he recognized as one of his. The shirt was not buttoned and when she leaned over to deliver the cup of coffee to him, he noticed just how shear her nightgown was. It was a short gown, and her legs looked bare under his shirt. Her breasts were all but pouring out of the gown's shear top. He could see now just what type of nipples she had. His manhood, as if it had a mind of its own, stiffened.

"Could you button up?" he said to her while averting his eyes from her seductive cleavage.

She smiled at him and then did a reverse striptease; she hummed the striptease tune while slowly buttoning the shirt—his shirt—from the bottom up, leaving the top open just enough for some cleavage to tease his eyes.

Steve shook his head in a frustrated way and then added in a slightly demanding tone, "What did you mean last night by you can't sleep alone? I thought you were living on your own in an apartment in town. Who are you sleeping with?"

As soon as those words left his mouth, he felt like he had over-stepped his bounds. He felt like he had come off too informally, as if he had some right to know. They had just met yesterday, and previously he couldn't have imagined that he would ever actually meet her. He was still uncertain how he fit in her life, if at all. He was just about to utter, "Sorry. That's none of my business," but she responded, "I do have to sleep alone most nights. But I do have boyfriends; I'm not a virgin. In fact, I wasn't one before the abduction. I was nineteen, you know. Now I can drink and make love." Steve was again floored that she was so cavalier about the incident. She had no qualms using the term "abduction" to describe it.

"Do you currently have a boyfriend?" he asked in a less demanding tone.

"Nothing serious, a fuck-buddy or a friend with benefits, but he's not someone I would end up with, that's for sure."

Her use of the word fuck-buddy hung in his mind. Steve thought of himself as sexually progressive, he always had. But now, hearing Tara speak that way, he suddenly felt odd, as if his prowling days were slipping behind him and the next generation was talking up the charge—even though he was only six years older than Tara. He still saw her as the missing Pine Teen.

"You're an amazing young lady, Tara," he said between sips of coffee.

"What is it about me that you find so amazing?" she quizzed him.

"Everything. But mostly your ability to have seemingly put behind the horrific things that happened to you, and talk about it as if it happened to someone else. I mean, have you put it behind you? Are you just putting on a brave face? Have you ever talked to anyone, a psychologist or anyone like that?"

"Yes, of course . . . I've spent time with several

psychologists. But I've done more than that, Steve. I've started and continue to run a weekly support group for troubled girls. Well, it started out for girls, but we now have women of all ages . . . so, it's a support group for women . . . all types of trouble like domestic violence. We even do modeling. I'm confident you will see what I am talking about someday soon."

Steve looked at her with admiration but still felt odd about her being in his home.

"I'm really well-grounded now. I sense that you have a hard time believing me, but I've done the work. I'm OK. You don't need to worry about me, at least in this matter...Anyway, what about you? Why no girl-friend?" She suddenly turned the inquisition to him.

"What gives you the impression I don't?"

"There's no evidence of a woman living here, or even crashing here for that matter. And it's a weekend. You've easily accommodated my sudden arrival. If you had a girlfriend, there would have been some mention of a change of plans or something."

"I'm between things," was all he said. But her observant questioning shifted his thoughts to himself. He didn't have a good answer to why he stopped dating altogether. He couldn't come up with a good answer for that question, not for himself, not for his friends who always asked, and certainly not now for Tara.

After breakfast, Tara headed into the bathroom to take a shower. As Steve sipped his coffee, his thoughts once again returned to the incident. He recalled the details he had learned about how the police solved the case and found Tara still alive. Some of the details of the case he had learned from Jane—his intimacy with her opened more than just her legs—and some from the police sergeant himself—he had shared a few beers with the sarg at the Pine Arms after the rescue—and some from the rumor mill around town. He started daydreaming about what a crap shot it had been that the camera was able to capture the mirror flying off the truck. And how it captured the key clue.

The reason the case was cracked.

6

Case Cracked

T he Pembleton camera only provided the police with pictures of the truck's mirror, and the last picture clearly showed its part number. With the part number, they concluded the truck was a Ford F150 between the years 1960 and 1970. That same mirror was used throughout those model years. But where to look from there? There were hundreds of thousands of F150s registered in New York, tens of thousands from those years alone. Without a plate number, the police had a tall order investigating the whereabouts of that many trucks. And, given the number of vacationers and other transients in and out of White Pine at any given time, the police wouldn't necessarily be looking at a local resident. That truck could have come from anywhere, even out of state.

Another week had gone by and Sergeant Tim called Steve several times during that week to ask him if he remembered any of the license plate numbers.

"No. I'm terribly sorry. I would only be guessing," he would say every time. Each call from Tim only made him feel worse for not remembering the plate number.

"Well, keep trying. We got a lead on the make and model of the truck, but we really need to narrow it down. That plate number—actually, any of the numbers, if you can remember just a few—will help enormously," Sergeant Tim reminded Steve. During this particular call, the sergeant was just about to hang up the phone, when he said, "Wait, I've got an idea. Have you ever been hypnotized?"

"No. Not that I recall," Steve replied.

"It's worth a shot. I'll set up an appointment with a shrink we have worked with before on this sort of thing, where a witness can't remember a key event. I'll call you back with the details. Stay by your phone," Tim barked the order to Steve as he hung up the phone. The hypnosis was a success. While under, Steve recalled the whole intersection encounter with remarkable lucidness. He not only recalled two digits and two letters of the license plate number, he was able to give a more detailed description of the man driving the truck. The plate numbers Steve recalled were 5 and 8, and the two letters were A and C. This was enough to narrow the truck down to two individuals in New York that owned a green Ford F150 in that year range. For some reason, yet unknown to Sergeant Tim, the description Steve gave of the driver did not match what the DMV had on file for either one of those two truck owners. The state police immediately dispatched two units to find and question the owners of those two trucks.

One lead proved to be a dead end. The owner of that truck had had his truck in his possession at the time and date of the incident, and he was at work all day with his truck parked in the parking garage. His alibi checked out.

As for the other truck owner, the police had a little more work to do to get to the bottom of that mess.

A month before the intersection incident, John Dexter, a guy with a shady past and a long rap sheet, was released from prison. He had been convicted of endangering the life of a woman, a woman who was eighteen at the time, for which he spent a year in jail.

The DA wanted to convict him on pimping and pandering charges, but they couldn't prove it. The woman, a friend of the Dexter family, wouldn't talk. They did prove that the woman, while in Dexter's care, was exposed to alcohol, drugs, and prostitution.

So, up to the penitentiary John went. After he served his time, John moved back in with his childhood friend and wanted to get away from everything for a while, and he told his friend that "he set his life straight." He had some money he would stash in his bedroom from drug deals he did before he was sent up to the pen, and he used this money to buy a truck from a drug addict he had previously sold drugs to. Kurt, the drug addict, needed money for drugs, and he was all too eager to sell his truck for a fix. Neither the drug addict, Kurt, nor the ex-con, John, thought to get the legal transfer paper work done on the truck. Neither respected the DMV or the state's authority in the matter. They weren't smart enough to care one way or the other.

When the cops descended on Kurt at his home, they found him stoned out of his mind. They arrested him and took him in for questioning.

"Where's your truck? And where were you on June 23, at 12:16 p.m.?" They badgered him for hours.

Finally, Kurt gave up John Dexter. He told the cops about the truck he had sold to him a month earlier, and that they didn't do any of the transfer paperwork. He had just taken the money and given Dexter the keys.

Believing that Dexter, after his release from prison, was again living with his friend, Jason, the SWAT team descended on Jason's home. Bashing in the door, they demanded to know where John was. John had previously told Jason he would be staying in the Adirondacks and would be renting a cabin in the town of Pine Hill, a neighboring town to White Pine. In his mind, there was no need to tell him where he was going. After all, he was going up there to, as he put it, "set his life straight". He was not planning to commit another crime while away at the cabin, nor anytime in the future as far as that goes. He had thought that he was done with jail and was looking for a fresh start.

But John's worst devils got the best of him.

A month into his self-prescribed seclusion, John Dexter got restless. The cabin he had rented was off the grid, and the only way to it was a mile-long dirt road. John himself couldn't say why he had gotten in his truck that June day and gone into the town of White Pine. He was looking for something, something only the deep recesses of his lizard brain understood.

When he saw a young woman hitchhiking along a county road outside of town, he spun the truck around. Tara had been warned against hitchhiking many times by her mother, but she always brushed it off.

She and her friends had hitchhiked all the time into town and the few miles home again.

Usually, locals picked them up and they had a nice chat during the ride. A good way to catch up on gossip in a small town. No harm had ever come of it. She didn't recognize the truck that pulled over to pick her up, but she got in anyway. When John didn't make the turn Tara had told him to take to get to her house, she began to suspect something was wrong.

Within a few miles, the truck careened through the intersection where Steve had been running.

The cops radioed ahead to the Pine County barracks. An all-out SWAT team descended on the cabin John was renting. Helicopters and dogs were deployed.

They caught John red-handed at the cabin. Tara was locked in a bathroom. The dogs attacked John as he tried to escape; they bit him in his crotch, subduing him. John tried to reach for a gun. The SWAT team loaded a dozen bean bag pallets on John and tazed him. The SWAT team placed him under arrest and took him to custody, saving Tara.

As Steve sat there after breakfast finishing his coffee while Tara showered, he imagined the dogs cornering that creep in the woods as the ex-con tried to escape; one dog biting his crotch, three other dogs barking in his face as that monster squirmed on the ground trying to protect his dog-bitten privates.

The sounds of the dogs barking in Steve's head while he daydreamt of Tara's past nightmare obscured the sounds from the bathroom. He didn't hear the shower turn off, or a few minutes later, the bathroom door open. When Tara came down the hall and back into the kitchen, she was drying her hair with a towel. She had another towel wrapped tightly around her body. Steve, startled by her seemingly sudden appearance in the kitchen, was caught off guard. The unmistakably beautiful form of her body under the tightly wrapped towel lured his lust from his control. Images of ripping the towel off her and devouring her with his tongue flashed momentarily through his mind. He undressed her with his eyes and fantasized about her in his mind. Steve once again remembered who she was and what she had gone through. He suppressed his erotic thoughts, but not before those brief thoughts hardened his penis. Steve started to wonder, why is she still here? What does she really want? Something is not right with this girl.

As Tara continued to tangle her hair, she moved closer to where Steve was sitting at the table. As his penis was getting hard, he said to himself, "This girl is crazy."

"What are we going to do today?" she questioned. He had given this some thought during breakfast. He knew he would have to entertain her for the weekend. He was making a mental list of things to keep them busy—too busy to let his lust win over his will. Steve wanted to find out Tara's motives for spending time with him.

"What are we doing?" Steve questioned back. Tara's phone kept on going off from a bunch of text messages. Steve thought it must be Tara's mom since she didn't go to work and was missing again.

"Shouldn't you answer that? It sounds like it's important. Is it your Mom?"

"Don't worry about it. Everything is going to be just fine. So, you didn't answer my question. What are we doing today?" Tara said, still wrapped in a towel and drinking coffee.

Knowing he wasn't going to win this battle, Steve came up with a quick answer.

"I thought we could take a train into the city. We can shop, or just walk around and sight-see . . . get some dinner, or something. I don't imagine you've spent much time in the city. Have you?"

"No. I've only been there once. Just last year, in fact. A few of my girlfriends and I spent a weekend there for my twenty-first birthday. Girls Gone Wild in NYC we called it, but it was kinda lame and shitty. We just shopped like crazy. No one got laid or showed their tits."

She finished drying her hair and then flipped her hair back and tossed the hair-drying towel at Steve playfully.

"Or we could stay here and spend all day in bed," she said with a devious grin, and then she let the towel wrapped around her body slip from her and to the floor. She finessed a lame attempt to cover herself and make it look like the towel slip was accidental.

"We're not doing this, Tara. I meant what I said." But not before he got a full frontal view of her naked body. He was at war with himself. He wanted to be good with her; to be her rescuer, her protector, but he had not been with a woman as beautiful as Tara in a very long time. Her sweet, sexy slim body tempted his libido. Her shaved tunnel of love looking so pink and juicy. Steve couldn't help but get aroused as he slightly rubbed his body parts. Trying not to let Tara notice he wanted her body bad. She pouted as she picked up the towel and headed to the bedroom to get dressed. She didn't bother covering herself as she walked away, her bare ass moving down the hall. Steve felt his lust rising. He shook his head in an attempt to eliminate those stimulating thoughts. Instead, he went to the bathroom and massaged himself to control his horny thoughts.

On the train ride into the city, Tara leaned against him with her head on his shoulders. He felt the warmth of her body pressed against his. He smelled the sweet scent of her hair, and for a moment, he let himself imagine they were together as a couple. He questioned his personal position on the matter. Why was he so strongly against the idea of having sex with Tara? She obviously wanted it. And she seemed very mature and horny for her age. He was the elder person only by about six years or so, but he felt a responsibility to her he couldn't quite grasp, and he started to doubt his own authority on the matter. This made him take a mental inventory of where he was in his life. He took a trip down memory lane, and in his mind, he saw all his discarded ex-girlfriends looking disapprovingly at him. Where he would once see himself as a playboy, sampling women in a noncommittal lifestyle, now alone at twenty-eight, he started to get a sense of the loss he perpetrated on himself and others. He thought of the two ex-girlfriends he had actually fallen in love with. One in particular that he had often thought about, and he daydreamt of them married and with a child.

For a moment, he thought, If the child was a daughter, would she grow up to be like Tara? She could do worse than to grow up as mature and level-headed as Tara, he mused. But this only endeared him more to Tara. As the train rumbled toward the city, he thought briefly of a baby made between the two of them. Again, Tara's phone kept going off and off. Phone call then text. Whoever it was, she would text back.

"Are you sure you're OK?" Steve asked, getting a little worried. He was now all alone with a girl that may have run away from home again, but this time, she was twenty-two.

"I'm fine. Just got fired from that bullshit job I had." Tara laughed. "I'm good spending my time with you."

Steve's phone rang. It was Jane. Steve's chest and heart felt like a panic. Did she know he was with Tara? Was Tara reported missing again? Or did she want some more time to make love? A booty call in his mind. All these thoughts ran through Steve's head as he sent the call to voicemail.

"Now who was that?" Tara demanded playfully. "Oh, just a friend. Nobody important," Steve said, sounding a little nervous. Jane left a voicemail. Then a text. "**Call me ASAP**," it read.

It started to rain while they were walking through the city, so they ducked into a bookstore to wait it out. The bookstore doubled as a coffee shop. They both ordered espresso drinks, him a cappuccino, her a caramel cloud macchiato, and then settled into perusing the bookshelves. Though he had an e-reader, Steve loved bound books. "There's just something more I get from reading a real book, it's more tangible, I can feel the essence of the words on the page," he said to Tara as he picked up a book and smelled the binding.

"Ah . . . I've been hearing good things about this author, and I'd like to read a few chapters to see if I like his style," Steve said as he motioned to a Lay-Z-boy chair where he wanted to park himself for a while. Tara found something to read and parked herself in an adjacent chair.

After reading two chapters of Dark Obscurity by Bradley Cornish, he fell in love with this author and was very much in love with the book. He looked up and saw Tara reading in the chair next to him. He saw something of Tara's mother in her face, especially her lips; those lips of her mother's that he had intimately become familiar with. Steve's mind drifted to Samantha's lips, and the day he met her . . . but again, Jane was calling him, and he didn't care to know why. He thought she just wanted some of him.

7

Samantha Murphy

It was mid-August, a month after the police SWAT team and their crotch-biting K-9s apprehended John Dexter and freed Tara. A blazing hot afternoon, and Steve had just finished showering after a sweaty run. He heard a knock on his cottage door. He wasn't expecting anyone. Jane and Steve were in a friends with benefits relationship, but Jane always texted before she came over. He wondered who it could be as he wrapped a towel around his waist and made his way to the front door.

"Hi. I hope I'm not disturbing you? My name is Samantha, Samantha Murphy. I'm Tara's mom. Can I come in? I would like to talk to you for a few moments."

Steve was taken aback. He wasn't prepared to

address anyone in Tara's family, let alone her mother. What if she was here to give him hell for not going to the police sooner than he had? He didn't really want to deal with that, but what could he have said to have gotten rid of her politely?

"Um . . . ah . . . yeah . . . I guess . . . come on in," he stammered.

Samantha entered the cottage and then extended her hand to him; they shook hands and exchanged greetings. At the time, Tara's mother was thirty-eight years old, thirteen years older than Steve at twenty-five, but she dressed younger than her age. His first impression was that she was barely getting away with wearing those clothes. As young and horny as Steve was, he always wanted to make love to a cougar, knowing he would screw her brains out. Her halter top was straining to contain what appeared to be naturally large breasts, and the short shorts she wore that day were too tight, and informed him that she was probably a sexually liberal woman. Overall, she looked to be in fairly good shape for her age, but motherhood had not left her unscarred. Her breasts looked like they might sag more than a fair bit if her halter top wasn't helping to support them. Her stretch-marked midriff sported a sexy small tummy bump, with some of it hanging over the waistband, and her thighs bulged a little out of the bottom of those hot pants.

"I've come to thank you for saving my daughter's life," Samantha said.

Steve felt the pains of guilt he had been carrying around for over a month in his gut. "I should have gone to police right away. I'm sorry . . ."

"But you did go to the police, and it saved her life. You are our hero," Samantha interrupted him as she moved closer and then knelt in front of him. Her movements shocked him for a moment. He thought she was bowing to him, as one would to worship a hero; after all, she did use the "hero" word. But when she raised her right hand and started massaging his thigh beneath the towel covering his crotch, he knew then exactly just what type of hero worship she had in mind.

"This is not necessary, Mrs. Murphy," he said as he took his left hand and pushed her hand away from his crotch and held her hand off to his side. She simply replaced her right hand with her left and continued to massage his strong runner's thighs as she smiled up at him and said, "You're not going to deny me my chance to properly thank you, are you, Steve? What's the matter? Is your girlfriend here?"

"No. She's not here, but that's not the point . . ." he started to say.

"I work in the District Atorney's office too, Steve. I'm a legal secretary there. I know you've been hooking up with Jane," Samantha interrupted with a big grin. "And I know she's in court today," she added, all the while massaging Steve's testicles beneath his towel with her left hand. "I hear you are a good lover!" Samantha said with a smirk.

He grabbed her left hand with his right and moved it out from under his towel and held it away from his crotch. His right hand had been holding the towel around his waist, so now the towel fell to the floor and his penis sprang up to Samantha's face.

Presented with the object she had come to thank, she simply extended her head forward and placed his joystick in her mouth while he continued to hold her two hands out to the side.

Once he felt the warmth of her mouth, Steve lost all of his self-control. "Well, I guess if you just have to thank me," he relented. He let go of her hands and placed his on the back of her head and caressed her blond hair as he gently guided her head in and out. She then reached for his balls with her right hand as she grabbed his ass with her left hand.

She pulled her mouth off him to catch her breath, and as she did, she moved her left hand to his joystick and massaged him gently while she continued to rub his balls with her right hand. When she returned her mouth to his body, she kept her hand on his shaft and stroked up and down, following her mouth as she pulled his swollen erection in and out. She drooled all over his muscular body and continued to massage him.

"I'm about to explode," Steve yelped.

She pulled off him. Panting, she said, "I can sense you're about to unleash a load in my mouth any moment."

She tore her clothes off and then slouched on the couch with her butt near the edge of the cushion, her feet near her butt, and her legs spread open. She played with her hair while Steve got on his knees and shuffled between her legs. He moved his head between her open legs and got to know her garden of love. He wasn't there long. She used her fingers to pull his head up and away from her flower. Steve looked at her, puzzled, as if he wasn't doing a good job teasing her. "Honey, normally I'd love to have you play with me. But I need you more than that," she added, removing his doubt.

He moved up and aligned his pulsating love muscle with her waiting juicy body. He planted his hips at her parted lips and then drove into her. He took his time to enjoy her. Besides, this was his dream cougar. He enjoyed the feeling of her silky wet lips and slipped into a smooth and easy rhythm.

"I want it fast and hard," she begged. He picked up the pace and started slamming into her pelvis. She grabbed his ass to assist his thrusts; he got the hint and pounded her even harder.

"Harder . . . " she begged as he slammed his hilt to her labia.

She signaled her orgasm first. Her moans and short breath set Steve in motion to deliver his own climax into the mix. Soon, they were screaming the orgasm song together—a duet of moaning, shuddering, and panting as they climaxed together.

Exhausted, Steve pulled out and released his juices on her breasts and chin before he collapsed on the floor, still panting. He couldn't understand why he felt so spent from just one moment of lovemaking. Something was settling in on him, some force, a blanket of self-reproach. Steve smiled. A cougar.

Steve woke up from his daydream to Samantha looking puzzled. "Sorry, what did you say again?" Steve asked. Samantha looked at him and smiled.

"Just wanted to thank you again for being in the right place at the right time. That's all."

The dream and the conversation stayed on Steve's mind for at least the next week, since he would be leaving the Adirondacks in late August to return to campus for the fall semester. He was still confused as to why Samantha came to him in the first place. Steve saw Samantha one more time that week for coffee as they got to know each other more. He felt there was something Samantha was hiding, but Steve just couldn't put his mind to it.

That curiosity would run through Steve's mind for the next few years. When he got back to campus that fall, he tried to resume his normal playboy life, but he was not the same. His dating suffered. He hopped from relationship to relationship but felt unfulfilled, the past always there—haunting him, interfering with his sex life, busting his ego. He chalked it up to getting old, even though he was still young. He thought his sexual prowling days were behind him.

There was always one thing that Samantha told Steve that he couldn't stop questioning.

"Tara was suffering from Stockholm Syndrome, and the truth will never be the same."

8

Stockholm Syndrome

"I'm sorry . . . I'm sorry . . . I can't . . ." Steve muttered, asleep in the corner bookstore chair as he dreamt of his last time with Samantha, that wet dream of intercourse.

"Steve . . . wake up . . . Steve . . ." Tara whispered as she shook him gently. "Your phone keeps ringing, someone is really trying to get a hold of you," Tara said curiously.

"What . . . ah . . . oh . . . I guess I dozed off a bit," he said as he blinked his eyes and came to. He checked his phone, it was Jane again and she left several voice-mails, but Steve didn't bother to listen to them.

"I guess that book is a winner then," she remarked sarcastically. "You were talking in your sleep. What were you dreaming about?"

Not wanting to disclose that he had been dreaming of her mother and the last time they had talked, or at least the last attempt that ended limply, he muttered, "Oh, nothing much . . . just some political shit going on at school; some administrative crap."

She didn't believe him but left it at that. The rain stopped, so they left the book store and resumed their day wandering the city. They visited a few art galleries and some boutique clothing shops where he bought her some new pants, a blouse, and a sexy little black dress, which she left on.

Tara in her little black dress, they walked the streets of the city. They found a quiet little place to have dinner. It was a little early for dinner and the restaurant was almost empty. They were seated in a quiet corner. "I need you to make love to me," Tara suddenly blurted out after they placed their order.

She had a way of dropping those bombs right when he least expected it, when there was a quiet lull in the conversation, when his mind was hanging onto another thought.

"Tara, I've already told you, no." As soon as the word "no" came out of his mouth, he felt as if he was someone else, a father telling a kid he couldn't have a toy. Again, he felt conflicted; he didn't want to be that guy.

"But you haven't really given me a good reason why not," she said. "I'm twenty-two and you're twenty-eight and it's not a big age difference. Are you just into older women, like my mother?" Tara smirked at Steve.

"Um . . . What does that mean? Besides, how is your mom anyway?"

Tara smirked again. "A little tied up right now."

Steve didn't say anything; he just looked at her peculiarly. His feelings were bouncing somewhere between irritated and turned on but puzzled. He couldn't tell whether he was irritated with her for continuing to bring it up, or if he was irritated with himself for not giving in to her. He couldn't quite grasp why he held this abstinence position so tightly when it came to her. He wondered if she somehow knew he was daydreaming of her mom at some point. This was not the circumstance he wanted things to be in, with him feeling like he was taking advantage of someone he rescued. Paradoxically, her persistence weakened his resolve, and he felt his lust swell within him.

"I do not need to be saved, Steve. I don't have a reverse savior complex, and you don't seem like the type that has the savior complex," she said, between sips of water.

"How do you know that?" he challenged her. "Because you would have already been in my life, trying to be my savior, a big brother, a father figure, or some shit. I wouldn't have had to come looking for you," she said. "My mother mentioned to me how she's tried to contact you several times. She said she surprised you the first time and you actually answered your phone. She told me that the two of you had a brief conversation, but that you didn't seem to want to be bothered. You wouldn't answer her other calls or call her back. She feels you're still suffering from guilt."

"You say you need to have sex with me. Why?" Steve questioned with curiosity.

"Because I fantasize about you. I didn't even know what you looked like, outside of my mother's description of you, but rather it's been the thought of you. I fantasize about the mystery man who saved my life making love to me. I want to stop fantasizing about it."

"So, you figure if we do it, you'll stop fantasizing about it?"

"That's the way it usually works," she said with a knowing smirk.

Trying to change the subject from the obvious, Steve added jokingly, "How do you know that I won't be so good in bed that you'll fantasize about me even more?" But then he felt stupid for making a joke at that moment.

"Well, then I'll have something real to fantasize about, not imagined. Look, Steve, I know I've said I'm well-grounded and all healed and stuff . . . from what happened. And I am, for the most part, but I still have a hole in my soul, and I need to heal . . ." she said, her voice trailing off and her eyes downcast.

She suddenly, for the first time, looked wounded to him.

"A hole?"

"Yes . . . it's not easy for me to explain." "Try me," he added.

Steve's phone rang again. Jane kept calling and Steve kept letting it go to voicemail.

"Well . . . as I said earlier, I wasn't a virgin before the abduction. And . . . this may shock you a little. . ." she paused, looking at him for any sign of disapproval.

He gave her a look that said, "Go on . . . I'm listening."

"Well . . . I used to like it . . . sex, that is. I always enjoyed sex. Before the abduction . . . before all that "

Tara said quietly and with a little blush. Her shoulders rolled in as she withdrew.

She received a text on her phone. Tara texted back and smiled in a way that made Steve uneasy.

"OK, that's nothing to be embarrassed about," he said.

"Well . . . I remember my struggles to keep that a secret. It's not easy for us girls to be ourselves in that matter, especially in high school. Boys want you to do things for them, but then they'll use it against you sometimes. It's pretty messed up, actually. It makes no sense. Other girls too, they're the worst. They'll brand you a slut and they don't give up . . . they're relentless," she added.

"Were you bullied in that way?" he asked.

"No. Not directly, but I had girlfriends that were. I was lucky enough to learn from them, and smart enough. Either that, or the boys I choose were nice, not assholes. Plus, I found someone that really understood me. Things got messed, but I'm going to fix them . . . it, I mean. Someone messed up my life and one day, sooner or later, they will get it." Tara smirked again. "Payback's a bitch, Steve. Remember that."

At this point, Steve really thought Tara had some screws loose and wanted to change the tone, but stayed on topic. "May I ask how old you were when you were bullied or got messed up?" he inquired uneasily.

He wasn't sure if that was something he should be asking her at that moment, or if it was any of his business at all.

"Seventeen," she replied, biting her lower lip and looking at him for any sign of disappointment. "Well, here's the thing . . . since the abduction, I have had nothing but bad memories about it. All I can do is think of that man, John Dexter. I have stress, nightmares, insomnia, and flashbacks of what happened to me with John."

"That's understandable given what you went through. But, I still don't understand how I fit in?"

Tara moved her gaze up from the table to Steve's eyes. She had a mildly painful but exasperated look on her face, as if her thoughts were telegraphing to him. "Just help me forget John. Don't make me have to explain this any further."

She took a deep breath and relaxed her composure before she continued. "So . . . look, Steve . . . you're part of that whole experience for me, whether you want to be or not. You're the good part. You set the wheels in motion that saved me, but you are, or were, just a fantasy to me. Up until now, I had no reality to ground you in that event. That's why I had to meet you.

And . . . this is hard to explain . . . but . . . I just feel . . . look, did you ever have anything go seriously wrong in your life, and then you have felt you needed to do something to offset that wrong? To take control and just do something that you have no control over?

I feel . . . I feel that I need you to make me forget,

to offset the bad memories from that . . . that awful time. You are the missing piece to my puzzle. When my mind drifts to that event, as it always will, I want to think of you, not him. I can't explain it . . . I just feel it in my gut . . . I just know it will help me close the wound."

Steve recalled his own tortured thoughts of his father, and how as a child he used to feel that if he could just meet him once, his father would see that he wasn't a burden, and everything would be fixed.

There was an awkward pause as he was lost in thought. She took this as disinterest.

"I'm sorry . . . I feel ashamed . . . I shouldn't have." she started to say before Steve interrupted.

"No, no . . . nothing to be ashamed of, Tara. Something you said made me think of my . . . never mind . . . it's not important now," he tried to assure her that he was paying attention to her.

Steve continued, "Shame can be a destructive emotion. One shouldn't feel ashamed about their sexual desires. Sexual desire is as natural as feeling hungry and without either, we humans wouldn't be here. Aside from procreation, sex is a strong desire for us to connect with those we love . . ."

As he spoke, a thought flashed through his mind and it brought him oddly back to his father. His whole life he'd had a strong desire to connect with his father. Was I searching for my father through my girlfriends? he asked himself, deep in thought. Was I conflating the two? Is this why I can't stay in relationships very long? The timing was poor, but these thoughts hung there, demanding to be examined. Unconsciously, once he was certain a girlfriend could not help him find his father, his desire to renew the search compelled him to move on, to continue the search elsewhere.

His complexion paled and he stared off to nowhere as his mind spun and his eyes disconnected from the world. He felt the rollercoaster weight of his thoughts. This revelation both enlightened him and burdened him. A veil had been lifted, and he felt instantly embarrassed that he hadn't seen this before. For too long, he had stumbled through relationship after relationship, and like a fool, he hadn't a clue about himself, his private motivations.

"Are you OK?" Tara asked.

He snapped out of his trance. He realized he had been rude. Tara had been pouring her heart out to him and he got lost in his own mind.

"Yes . . . yes . . . I'm fine. I'm sorry. I have to apologize. You were saying that you believe making love to me will help you heal . . . from what you went through. You're looking to replace the bad memories you now have surrounding sex with good ones," he said, attempting to smooth over his transgression of zoning out on her.

Tara smiled at him. "Sooo . . . you agree, then?"

He didn't answer her. He only smiled back. He felt that she took that as a yes, but he couldn't say no.

The waiter brought their main course. They stopped talking about it long enough to start eating and make small talk about the food.

"I'm curious," Tara began. "Go on," he prompted.

"Before the food came, you were talking about shame, and sexual desire, but then you got lost in thought. You were in deep. You were zoned out. What was going on back there?"

"Something in our conversation made me think of my father, and . . . and I think I just had some sort of breakthrough . . . it's stupid, but . . ."

"What? Tell me," Tara encouraged.

"I think my desire to find my father has produced an unnatural wanderlust in me. That unresolved conflict has been a destructive force that's bled into my relationships, especially my relationships with women, my love relationships."

"What did I say that made you realize that?" She asked.

"Nothing directly. The mind works in strange ways

sometimes. You were talking about your desire to right the wrong, and I was mentioning how sexual desire is a desire to connect with those we love and just . . . I don't know . . . those thoughts combined, and. . . weird . . ." he shook his head in disbelief that he had thought of it at all.

"See, we're good for each other," she said, smiling. "It makes me feel good that just talking to me was able to help you see that. Soon, I'm gonna make you see something else. You gonna be all tied up," Tara said, checking her phone and texting someone again. "Excuse me, I have to take this call." Tara left the table.

Steve watched her walk away, keeping his eyes on her ass. Steve was curious about the phone call, and then he remembered to check on Jane. As he went to his phone to call Jane back, Tara returned. "All ready?" she asked, grabbing his hand as though they were a couple. Steve put his phone back in his pocket as they walked to the train station.

On the train ride home, Tara leaned her head again on his shoulder and snuggled her body up to his.

He felt the warmth of her pressed against him. He felt her left breast press against his right arm. As the train made its way north to Steve's station, passengers disembarked at other stations along the route. No new passengers were getting on the train as it was late and everyone was going home from the city. In the dark, mile by mile, station by station, the train emptied. They sat near the back of one of the train cars.

When their section of the car emptied enough to offer privacy, Tara said, "I need you to do this for me. I don't want you to protect me, Steve. I want you to heal me." Her right hand moved to his chest and she let a finger wander to his left nipple. She slowly twirled her finger around his nipple through his shirt. This time, he didn't push her away. After their conversation at dinner, he knew he needed to help her with her quest, and perhaps he was starting to realize he needed this too. He needed to absolve himself of the guilt he had carried around with him for the last three years. He was beginning to think that this was a way for both of them to move forward. To close the final chapter.

When she felt no resistance from him, when he didn't push her away, she moved her hand down to his thigh near his crotch and started kneading his inner leg. Throughout the day, Steve had been slowly letting down his guard. He wanted her now as much as she wanted him. His groin was on fire, and with each squeeze of her hand near his epicenter, his arousal grew a little more until it was straining in his pants. As she slowly moved her hand in that direction, she felt the heat of his sexual organs. She reached his thigh and massaged them through his pants. He moved in his seat to relieve some of the pressure caused by his erection.

He moved his right arm around her shoulders and pulled her close to him. She then moved her hand to his hard abs and slowly massaged them while she kissed him. He let his right hand brush the side of her right breast near her armpit.

A train conductor opened the door at the other end of the car and looked around to see how many people were left in this car. There were only a few other passengers towards the front of the car and Steve and Tara near the rear. The conductor's sudden appearance dampened Steve's growing lust.

"Not here," he whispered to Tara. "We're almost at my stop."

She removed her hand from his pants.

In the car ride from the station to Steve's apartment, the heat of their passion was palpable, the air thick with sexual musk. No words were exchanged; there was nothing more to say. Their logical brains had disengaged. They had given control over to their libidos.

Inside Steve's apartment, they turned to one another, and like two magnets, they came together and kissed tenderly. They gazed into each other's eyes for a moment and then Steve, still with lingering doubt, said, "Are you sure?"

"I need you," was all Tara said, and they kissed again. A long, passionate kiss. He moved his hands to her buttocks, which he had wanted to grab all night. He slipped his hand under the little black dress and massaged her butt through her panties.

She dropped to her knees and fumbled his belt open and unzipped his pants. He assisted her and pushed his pants down to his knees. She pulled his boxer briefs down and exposed his large erection she had been massaging on the train. She stroked it a few times before tasting it. She let out a deep, satisfying, primal moan as she engulfed his inner thighs. The object of her quest had entered into her being. She played with him gently and slowly. Tara savored every inch of him like a long-awaited dessert.

But she wasn't there to give him oral satisfaction, she needed him inside her. She soon got up and led him to his bedroom. As he removed his clothes, she stripped off the little black dress and got into bed.

Naked, he climbed in bed and kissed his way from her feet up to her Victoria's Secret panties. He put his fingers in the waist band of her panties; she lifted her butt and he slowly removed them. As her seductive body came into view, his intention to take control made him more aroused. She was ripe and ready to burst with ecstasy.

While his tongue got to know her body, she leaned up and reached behind her and unclasped her bra. Tara pulled at his head with her fingers to signal Steve to move his face away from her body, just as her mother had done in his dreams. "I'm so ready for you, Steve," she moaned.

Steve kissed her belly seductively. He knew she wanted to dance, but with her big beautiful core now in front of him, those luscious farm-bred apples he had briefly fantasized about now spread out for him like a banquet, he just had to stop and savor her sweet cherries. She patiently let him devour her breasts as she reached down between his legs and played his emotions, sending him into a frenzy. She toyed with her body using the other hand.

The foreplay continued and Tara closed her eyes as her head slowly moved back onto the bed.

When she couldn't wait any longer, Tara pulled Steve closer to her heart. He positioned himself to get a deep look into her eyes and looked at her lovingly. Leaning over her, he kissed her softly. She responded with a slight moan. Biting his lips, holding him tightly while her legs wrapped around his body. Their kisses were soft and sweet, a getting to know you exploration of tender lips touching tender lips, and tongues communicating a love dance only their tongues understood.

Tara couldn't wait any longer, she wrapped her legs around his butt and pulled him into her deeper again. She closed her eyes and bit her lip in satisfaction. Tara covered her mouth with her hand as Steve slowly moved in.

"You OK?" he whispered. "I don't want to hurt you."

She nodded her head and smiled. He pushed in a little further and stopped. He looked into her eyes for direction. She extended her head up and kissed him. She whispered in his ear, "Please. Don't stop."

Steve closed his eyes as he entered her body. She let out a moan that sounded to Steve as if it came from the depths of her soul. Her skin flushed. Sweat started to leak through her nose. Tears welled in her eyes and leaked down her cheek. He kissed the tears off her cheeks and then moved his lips to her mouth.

Their salty lips tingled with electric sensations as they softly kissed.

Steve slowly and tenderly made love to Tara. He was not himself; he was having an out-of-body experience. He felt as if he could last for days inside her. Each stroke erased a little more of the guilt that had dogged him these past three years.

For Tara, each slow and steady stroke in and out comforted her. Each stroke healed the damage done three years ago. She felt whole again, her mission accomplished.

Slowly, their lust built with each passing minute. With each stroke, slowly, the warmth and comfort they first experienced turned into raw passion. Steve picked up his pace and Tara started to push onto him, meeting his body with hers as he drove his erection deeper into her. They began to moan in unison. Her whole body began to quiver and quake. Little currents of orgasm flowed within her from head to toe. His body pulsed inside her.

They wanted to stay like that forever, but they knew they couldn't deny the orgasm that was overtaking them.

Soaked in sweat, they breathed heavily as they looked into each other's eyes and smiled. They kissed again sweetly. He remained inside her while she wrapped her arms and legs around him, holding him there. They simply held each other and breathed. They rocked gently as one until a second, milder orgasm washed over them both.

Exhausted, he pulled out of her and rolled over on

his back. She snuggled into him with her head on his chest and her right leg wrapped over his. They both fell soundly asleep.

Again, Jane called Steve trying to get a hold of him.

With the morning light, and without a word, they both knew their passionate night was not to be repeated. The love that flowed between them was a special bond, not like a lover's love, or a familiar love. They were soldiers in the war of life. Circumstances beyond their control had collided their lives together. That night, they both had done what they needed to do to free themselves from the event three years ago that interrupted their lives, when they unknowingly crossed paths.

"I made coffee." Tara handed Steve a cup while he checked his phone.

"Oh, shit, I forgot," he said out loud, drinking the whole cup of coffee.

"Um, what did you put in this"? he asked.

Tara just stood and looked at him with an evil,

crooked grin as Steve listened to the first voicemail from Jane.

"Steve, John escaped from prison. Samantha and Tara are both missing. You need to call me."

Suddenly, Steve grew light-headed. The room was starting to spin and he fell unconscious.

9

The Set-Up

Splash . . . Splash . . . Splash. The sound of water hitting Steve's face as he sat tied up in a chair. Regaining consciousness, Steve opened his eyes to a tall, thin white man sitting across from him. He recognized the man immediately. It was John Dexter. "So, you're the so-called fucking hero, you motherfucker," John said, punching Steve in the face, making his nose bleed.

John punched Steve over and over again. Blood coming from his nose and mouth. His right eye swollen shut.

"Where is Tara?" Steve said in a soft stutter.

John laughed it off as he punched Steve again, this time in the stomach.

"You think she seduced you and gave you some ass. Y'all lovers now?" John said, lighting a cigarette.

"Hey, babe, he's asking for you," John yelled out towards the bedroom.

Tara walked in. This time, she didn't look as pretty.

"What the fuck do you want?" she said as she spat in Steve's face.

"What's going on?" Steve mumbled, barely able to stay awake.

"You fucked up everything with your going to the cop shit," John angrily yelled at Steve.

John continued, "Three years. Three years I spent in that fucking rotten jail because of you. You know they don't like my accused kind in prison. I didn't kidnap Tara. Tara wanted to be my bottom bitch. We had money dreams until you fucked it all up with your running ass."

Steve looked at Tara. "Why did you lie to me and make love to me?"

"John always told me payback's a bitch," Tara replied. She took a sip of water then continued, "You fucked up everything. My life, John's life. All because you wanted to run, you stupid motherfucker. While John was sitting in jail, you were getting praise from Jane and my mother. Getting pats on the back for putting away my lover. While you were cuddled up with my mom and having playdates. I bet she didn't mention I ran away because she kept beating me every night and I was fucking fed up with it. So, I met John that same day and we fell in love. I started working with him. Fuck you and fuck her. I'm getting the last laugh now."

"Love?" Steve jumped in. "That ain't love. He's using you and making a profit. He doesn't care about you. Just money. You are suffering from Stockholm Syndrome."

"Just like you, I've lost my dad. I lost my mom the first time she got drunk and started beating me. John took me in and loved me. And no! It wasn't sexual love. Everyone thought we had sex. He was the father I had always wanted and never had. I will kill for him, and he would do the same for me and the others," Tara said, smiling at John.

"Others?" Steve said in shock.

"You will see at the cabin. Let's wrap this shit up and go back to White Pine," John told Steve as he put a bag around his head to blind him.

"Don't tell me you are taking me to the same cabin you got busted in?" Steve said under the trash bag.

"What, you think I'm an idiot?" John barked back. "This one's way off the grid. No one will find us for days, and by that time, you'll be long dead."

"If you're gonna kill me, just do it right here. Why waste time taking me back to the cabin?" Steve shouted as he felt his heart jump out of his chest.

John laughed. "I've waited three years to fuck you up. I'm gonna enjoy this. Take my time and do it right. Plus, I have to show you what they did to me in prison. I have a baton with your name on it.

I'm gonna get all in your ass, boy," John laughed as he tortured Steve.

Boom, boom, boom. Three knocks on Steve's front door. "Who the fuck is that?" John asked, looking at Tara.

Tara walked up to the door to look out the peephole. "Steve, are you there?" The other voice outside yelled.

Tara rushed back to John in a panic. "It's that DA bitch, Jane," Tara said looking nervous. "We have to kill her," she added before John could finish gathering his thoughts.

John smiled as if he was having the best day ever. "Open the door and let her in. She's coming with us," John said as he opened the bag on his shoulder and pulled out a small handgun.

"Run, Ja—" Steve tried to yell before John pistol-whipped him and knocked him out.

"Get the door!" John instructed Tara as he moved behind the door.

"Do you want me to get rid of her?" She asked John.

"No, that bitch put me away like that fucker. She's coming with us. Today's my lucky day."

Tara opened the door to see Jane standing there shocked, looking at Tara.

"Tara?" What are you doing here?" Jane asked demandingly.

"Just seeing my hero, Steve, and making love to him. I mean, thanking him."

"Where is he?" Jane asked in frustration.

"He just got out the shower. Gotta wipe off that sex juice," Tara said with a smirk, knowing it would get under Jane's skin.

"It looks cold outside. Why don't you come on in? I will go get Steve and let him know you are here," Tara said as she turned her back to head to the other room.

Jane walked in, following Tara. The door closed behind her and John cocked the gun to Jane's head.

Jane turned around quickly. "John!" Jane yelled.

"Well, hello, bitch!"

10

The Drive

Y ou're a wanted man. Everyone's looking for you. Where's Steve?" Jane screamed frantically.

"I'm in charge now. Shut the fuck up!" John yelled as he pointed the gun to Jane's head.

John grabbed her by the hair and threw her down to the kitchen floor.

"Get the duct tape and another bag," John told Tara as he put his pistol in his waistband.

"Let's just kill them both now and get it over with. We can lie about it later," Tara replied eagerly with a smile.

"You fucked him in his bed. Your DNA is all over the place. The shower, sheets, and kitchen all comes back to you. They are coming to the cabin with us. It's perfect. Two love birds missing at the same time. Everyone would just think they're on a sexcapade."

Jane looked towards Steve's direction as he sensed her presence. "You fucked Tara? You sick motherfucker taking advantage of her. I should have not called you or been worried about you. Let alone bring my ass here to warn you about John. Now I'm in danger because of you. I'm going to die with you."

"It's not what you think." Steve tried to defend himself but was still too weak from the beating he took from John.

"Shut up! Both of you." John pulled out his gun again. This time, handing it to Tara.

"This is the play. Nothing's changed from the original plan. Shit just got better. Take this gun. Grab Jane's purse and keys and bring the car around back. Jane sits in the front with you, and I'll sit in the back with lover boy keeping an eye on them both."

Tara did exactly as she was told. Like she was under the control of John.

Tara took the keys out of Jane's purse and pressed the alarm button several times in many directions until she located the Ford Explorer that belonged to Jane. Tara noticed the vehicle had government plates with tinted windows. She sat in the vehicle and proceeded to drive around to the back of Steve's house that was adjacent to the alleyway. Tara entered the back door of the house and ran to John.

"We have a problem. The bitch got a government car. What if it's tracked?"

John put his right hand on his chin. Thinking of his next move. From the corner of his eye, he spotted Jane whispering something to Steve.

John rushed over and pistol-whipped Jane. "I said shut up, bitch. This ain't no family reunion. This is the John Dexter show."

Jane fell to the floor with blood dripping from her head. Steve jumped to her aid and defense, and John pistol-whipped him also. "Sit your bitch ass down before I put your mind next to hers so we can hear your thoughts," John said, waving his pistol.

John thought again about his plan to go to White Pine. He lit a cigarette and paced back and forth. He turned to Tara finally after taking his last puff.

"It's a government-issued car. Unless we drive over the speed limit, we shouldn't get caught. No one will notice Jane missing until after we get a chance to dump the car. I'll take Steve in the back seat, and you will take Jane in the front," John told Tara as he grabbed Steve by the arms to escort him out of the kitchen to the waiting SUV in the back.

Tara followed John, holding Jane tightly. Suddenly,

Jane reacted to being bigger than Tara and pushed her out of the way, yelling and making noise in the alley to get someone's attention.

Tara took the gun John gave her and shot Jane in the thigh, making her fall a few feet from the SUV.

"What the fuck! Making too much noise. Go get her and let's go before the cops come or someone notices," John yelled at Tara as he got in the car with Steve.

Tara ran to Jane and picked her up as Jane cried in pain after being shot in the thigh that was only a flesh wound. Tara escorted her back to the car as Jane limped all the way, holding the back of her left thigh.

"Oh, come on! It's only flesh. Stop your bitching. Karma's a bitch. You caused me three years of pain. Look what you get," John ranted as Tara started the drive to White Pine.

"If we're going to White Pine, it's a five-hour drive. I'm going to bleed out and die before I get there. I need medical help now," Jane cried as she turned to John.

"Bitch, please." John reached in his black bag and handed her a towel. "Hold this to your leg. It will stop the bleeding; it's only a fucking flesh wound."

"Says the guy with a jail medical degree," Steve mocked John's decision.

John chuckled. "You know, I've learned a lot and

lost a lot being in jail. I don't know if I should thank you or hate you."

"Then why are you doing this to me?" Steve asked furiously.

"There is a lot you need to know. You will just have to wait until we get to the cabin in White Pine. This is bigger than what you have imagined."

Five hours seemed like an eternity for Jane and Steve as they sat and waited for their fate. Steve sat there thinking of how this was the worst weekend of his life. He got screwed and seduced by Tara for this plan of hers and John's. Now, all of the weird phone calls and texts on Tara's phone made sense. This was the plan all along. Tara and John's revenge.

The car went silent while Tara drove to the White Pine border.

"Welcome to White Pine. Where it all begins, I should say," Tara yelled happily as Jane saw the sign welcoming residents and tourists along the two-lane highway. The car approached the same intersection that ruined Steve's run three years ago.

Suddenly, a tractor-trailer approached on the opposite side in the dark, lonely road.

"Now," Jane yelled as she took the steering wheel from Tara and forced the car to drive head-first into the oncoming truck.

Steve tried to wrestle John in the back seat to take away his gun.

He was still too weak to take on John, so John managed to out-muscle him and push him against the door. Steve hit his head on the window, shattering the glass and cutting his forehead. John leapt into the front seat as the truck was approaching the SUV and forced the car to the curb, crashing into a tree. The truck honked its horn and the driver stepped on the brakes, screeching its tires. Tara hit her head on the steering wheel, and Jane fell forward, hitting her head on the dash.

The truck driver got out of his truck, rushed over to the SUV to help render aid like a good Samaritan. John got out of the car.

"What the fuck? Are you guys all right?" The truck driver asked John after meeting him in the middle of the street.

"We're fine. But not for you." John took out his pistol and shot the truck driver in the head.

With Tara still unconscious, Steve woke up and witnessed John executing the driver in cold blood. He watched John standing over the truck driver's lifeless body. Steve quietly opened his side of the car door and went to Jane's door and shook her to wake up. Jane slowly came to her senses. Steve placed his hand over her mouth and made a quiet sound with his index finger. He pointed to John in the middle of the street as he placed the dead truck driver back in his truck. Steve and Jane entered the woods. Just as they reached the bushes, John noticed their attempt to escape and fired shots in their direction.

"So, it's a hunting trip now," John told himself as he lit a cigarette while walking back to the SUV.

"Tara, Tara. Get your ass up. They're trying to escape," John yelled as he shook Tara in the driver seat. "Wha—what happened?" Tara finally came back to her senses.

"You let them get away. That's what the fuck happened. Now, let's go get them bastards." John ran after his victims.

Tara was right behind John as they ran through the thick White Pine woods, the sun beginning to set.

"You know Steve is a runner. He's probably way gone by now," Tara said as she slowed down, running out of breath.

"Yeah, but you hit that bitch in the leg. Luckily for us, you are a bad shot. Plus, he's hurt too. They ain't going far." John got on one knee to look at the fresh footprints and the bloody trail Jane left from her thigh. He looked around the grass like a hunter and saw another bloody trail. "This way. They can't be far."

Steve and Jane were moving as fast as they could with Jane limping all the way with her injured leg.

"Steve, I'm tired. I need a break," Jane cried as they reached a small river that separated the woods.

"We need to keep going, Jane. They are going to kill us when they get a chance. This is our only chance for survival."

"I can't go on. I'm hurt and tired. I don't run like you do. I don't have the energy. Just fucking go without me."

Steve took Jane by the hand and looked her in the eyes, wiping her tears as they fell down her cheek.

"I'm not going anywhere without you. We are in this together," he said as he picked her up off the ground.

The sky started to turn pink. The wind chill was dropping and they could hear wolves howling in the background.

"We have to cross this river, I think. I don't know where we are going, but we must keep moving. They may be right behind us," Steve said to Jane as he surveyed the area.

"Not so fast, motherfuckers." John caught up with Steve and Jane with Tara slowly catching up behind. John waved his gun like he was in the wild west.

"I guess we're walking the rest of the way," John said as he motioned to the river for the party to cross.

"I . . . I need to rest." Jane sat on a log next to the river to catch her breath.

Steve managed to gain some courage to step up in Jane's defense. "We are staying right here. Fuck you, John. We're not moving any further. This shit stops right here."

"Oh really, tough guy? I don't like your snitching bitch ass anyway," John said as he raised his pistol. He shot Steve and Jane screamed. Steve's body fell back into the river. John blew on the barrel of his pistol and smiled as he saw Steve fall.

Tara ran next to John.

"Is he . . . Is he dead?" Tara asked.

Jane turned to the river. "Steve, Steve, Steve, get up!"

11

Cabin Fever

A passerby notified the police about the truck and SUV being on the side of the road. Police arrived and started a crime scene investigation.

"Ping." An alert sounded on Professor Pembleton's phone while he was at home grading papers. He finally had the ability to have all alerts from the camera at the intersection instantly. "Oh, what now? Another person ran a red light again," he said as he opened his phone to view the camera. The camera showed the near-miss accident and the murder and body placement of the truck driver, but it didn't show the escape attempt of Steve and Jane.

"Oh, shit! I have to notify Tim right away," James told himself as he dialed his number. They had become close friends since the first case three years ago and had helped each other since the Tara Murphy case.

"James! I was just about to call you. You have no idea where I'm at right now," Sergeant Tim expressed. "The same exact spot where my camera helped solve the case of Tara Murphy," James replied right away.
"Wow, you are on top of it like always, James. Sounds like you have some clues for us. What do you have?"

"Well," James hesitated. "I see a near-miss accident, and the SUV gets out of view. Then the truck driver is met in the middle of the street. But . . . I don't know if I could believe my eyes, Tim. The shooter . . . looks a lot like John Dexter, Tim. John fucking Dexter. This can't be right, can it?" James asked nervously.

"Unfortunately, it may be the case. John escaped from Bare Hill Correctional Facility two weeks ago. The media is not aware because Senator Smith wanted to keep this low-key due to the nature of the powerful case it was three years ago. Plus, his presidential campaign is going strong. Does the camera show where John went? Was he alone?"

"You mean to tell me there is a cult sicko out on the

loose and no one knows it? Whose fucked-up idea was that? But to answer your question, Tim, he went out of the camera view towards the SUV, but I don't see the SUV getting back on the road or anyone else."

"The SUV is still here. That helps a lot. I'm guessing he is in the woods trying to escape. I will get a search party started. Thanks, James. Stay by your phone and work on getting that footage to the station for evidence," Sergeant Tim told James.

"Ok, Tim. I will work on it now," James replied as they both hung up the phone.

"Sarge, we have an update and some bad news on the SUV." Officer Hayes handed over a document before he continued. "It seems the SUV is registered to DA Jane Goodwright. I called her office and her cell phone. No one can reach her, and no one has heard from her in the last few hours."

"All right, listen up. Gather around," Sergeant Tim announced as the crime scene team and the officers surrounded him.

"We have a possible escaped convict and a kidnapped

DA. It is this guy's motive to kidnap women to marry him for his cult, or whatever he likes to do. We need to search the surrounding woods for evidence and try to catch this bastard before it's too late.

Deep inside the woods, John heard a helicopter flying overhead. Jane continued to scream, "Steve, Steve, get up!"

John walked over to the river. Picked Steve up by the collar of his shirt as Steve tried to gasp for air.

"It's just a flesh wound to his shoulder. He's going to survive. At least for now, that is. Stop your bitching, Jane."

"We have to go, John. I think the cops are looking for us," Tara told John as he stood over Steve.

"All right, thanks to Jane. We are walking from here. Let's move, and don't slow us down. Your shoulder will survive, and so will your leg." He told them both.

"We don't know where we are going," Jane yelled as Tara grabbed her by the hair to help her on her feet. "I will lead. You will follow. Tara, stay behind and watch them. This time, if they fuck around, shoot 'em in the head," John said as he started to cross the knee-deep river.

"Even Steve? I thought we needed him alive." Tara asked John as the three followed him through the river.

"I will deal with Steve and the consequences," John said as he started the journey through the deep woods.

Steve was worried and curious. Pain was setting in on his shoulder. What is going on? He wondered. Why do they want me and for what? What do they want from me and where are we going? Steve questioned himself as his shoulder was bleeding heavy through his shirt. Over and over, the thought kept on going through Steve's mind.

The woods were getting darker and the chill in the air was getting colder as the four kept a steady pace deep in the forest, headed to their destination. Coyotes, wolves, and cougars could be heard in the distance while unknown creatures kept running around the blood of Steve and Jane.

Steve and Jane held each other for warmth and comfort. The butterflies in Steve's stomach made it hard for him to speak to Jane to console her. He was scared for himself. Afraid to die when he got to wherever they may be heading. It seemed like hours went by, and they kept walking with no breaks.

Jane's feet were starting to get numb as she finally broke the silence. "Steve, I don't know how much longer I can stand. My leg hurts. My feet are cold and I can't feel my toes," Jane said with a small tear running down her cheek.

"How much further do we have to go? Jane needs to rest and it's cold out here," Steve shouted to John.

"Shut your bitch ass up and keep moving. This is my show. We stop when I say we fucking stop," John said without missing a beat, smoking a cigarette.

"Well, can we at least get a cigarette?" Steve asked, holding onto Jane to keep her warm.

"All right, everyone stop. Let's have a small smoke break so Steve can feel like Superman," John announced as he handed everyone a stick.

"You know, we wouldn't be walking if someone didn't grow some balls and try to cause an accident, then make me kill some random punk trying to be a superhero and then two idiots trying to run off into the fucking woods," John yelled at the top of his lungs out of frustration.

"You are just a shithead. Why can't you just escape and leave us alone? What do you want from us?" Steve confronted John.

"Easy, tough guy. I don't care about you. You were specially requested by someone higher than me. As for Jane, well, she just happened to be in the right place at the right time," John said with a nasty smirk. "Now, let's get moving, bitches."

A t the police station, Sergeant Tim and James finally viewed the evidence of the murder committed by John.

"Yup, that's fucking John Dexter, all right," Tim said as he zoomed in on the camera. "I just can't tell if Jane is with him or not."

"Why would he come all the way back to White Pine when he got caught the first time?" James asked.

"Beats the hell out of me, but we need to get this son of a bitch. This time, he may not make it to jail,"

Tim told James as he closed the computer.

"What do you mean by that?" James questioned, shocked.

"Oh, you know. Cons don't wanna go back to jail. So, they would do whatever it takes to not go back. He may be looking for a fight this time. I doubt he is in the same cabin we caught him at last time. The last three years have changed the woods."

"So, what's your plan?" James asked, now a little more intrigued by the situation.

Sergeant Tim leaned back in his office seat and placed both hands behind his head. "At this point, he could be anywhere. With anyone. We must resume the search in the morning with SWAT and the K-9 units. If you can get anymore feed from your high-tech cameras, you know it's always helpful."

"Yes, sir. I will get on it first thing in the morning," James said as he walked out of the office.

John, Steve, Jane, and Tara walked for two days through the Adirondack Mountains, sunlight starting to blaze their eyes on the morning of the third day. Steve and Jane were getting more fatigued by the minute. John stopped to light a morning cigarette.

"Aww, I just love the smell of Logger's Loop Trail," he said as he blew smoke in Steve's face.

"How much further do we have to go? We have been walking for fucking days," Steve said angrily while helping Jane to her feet. At this point, the crew walked miles deep in the Adirondack Mountains. Jane's feet were swollen as the dried blood on her leg started to stain her skin.

"Where are we?" Jane muttered, wondering why the sudden stop after the momentum was starting to build.

"Well, whose idea was it to play superhero, mother-fucker? This is home. A place so desert that nothing grows here that we don't want to grow. Since the great fire of Adirondack. We are so far off the grid, the grid needs a grid. This is how we had survived all these years. Where I was taking Tara to be my partner in crime, before we got stopped at our little pit stop three years ago, thanks to this bitch ass," John said as he pointed his pistol at Steve for intimidation.

"Bullshit! You kidnapped her, and now you have her brainwashed in some sick mind game you're playing," Jane yelled at John.

"No way was she going to be part of any plans with you. You had her tied up and you wanted to have your way with her. I heard how terrified she sounded in that car," Steve chimed in to back Jane up.

John giggled and looked at Tara. Tara smiled back as she was in love.

"Is that what you really think? Let's just get this straight. Right here and right now. I may have had a little too much to drink when I picked up Tara after she ran away from her abusive mother. So, I may have almost flipped a bitch hitting the corner too fast. I wanted to impress my new girl with my new ride. Finding us in a cabin with her tied up…" John smiled from ear to ear before he continued while holding back a laugh.

"Who doesn't like a little BDSM and foreplay, huh?" John laughed while looking at Tara.

"You're right, baby," Tara replied, walking to John and giving him a hug.

"Going to jail was my choice. I didn't want the truth to come out about Samantha beating Tara and Jane going to child protective services. I would have never seen her again." John looked into Tara's eyes as if they were really lovers, giving each other a brief hug.

"I love my baby," John expressed in a soft tone, kissing Tara on the forehead.

Tara smiled back and looked John in his eyes. "Like you have always said, baby, the truth will shine someday."

"And today's the day," John replied, smacking Tara on the ass.

Steve didn't know what to do or say. He just looked down in guilt.

Steve started to feel bad, wondering if John was telling the truth. How could he send Tara back to an abusive mother? Jane looked at Steve and saw how disappointed he looked.

"You did the right thing. You didn't know Samantha was abusive. Neither did I." Jane hugged him.

"Thank you. I guess." Steve said, emotionless.

"Well, we're home," John said as he walked towards a bush between two Adirondack trees. It was like a magical city that appeared right before their eyes. The view that was seen by Steve and Jane blew their minds. In the distance was a small lake. The lake was the center of what looked like a small village. A town of what Steve picked up right away were beautiful women. They were all wearing the same type of clothing. It reminded Steve of a sexy Amish cult community. This time, all the women that Steve saw made him fall in love.

"What is this place?" Steve asked, trying not to stutter his words.

"We call this Breitenbush of White Pine," John said with his arms in the air like he was the holy savior. The king of all the land.

"Breitenbush? Like Breiten? Steve Breiten?" Steve asked in a state of shock. John and Tara smiled at each other, then smiled at Steve.

"Follow me so I can take you to where you will be staying. You have a big day tomorrow, Steve," John said as he walked down the hill headed toward the lake.

"I don't get what's going on. Why is this named after my last name?" Steve asked Jane.

"How the hell should I know? Are you sure you're not part of this sick shit?" Jane questioned back in a stern tone.

As they followed John to their destination, John

started to ramble. "A little history lesson for the newbies. This place was founded by our great leader almost thirty years ago today. Which was my father, if you didn't know. The Adirondack Mountains, where White Pine is located, are unique because of the abundance of lakes, ponds, rivers, and streams that crisscross the nature preserve. Approximately 30,000 miles of waterways run through the Adirondack Region. Where it is hard to find by locals and has plenty of fish, game and other natural resources to stay hidden for decades. No Google maps can locate this terrain. Hence the reason it took three days on foot to get here. The trees keep the sun out, and we can't be seen from the sky. A real hidden gem in White Pine. The best part of it all is that the land is privately owned by those of us that live here. So, it's legit in a way and we stay off the radar."

"Then why do you call it Breitenbush?" Steve asked curiously, wanting to know why this off the grid place carried part of his last name.

"Stop asking fucking questions. You shall find out tomorrow, I believe."

As they walked through the town, the locals all stopped to get a glimpse of Steve.

"Is that Steve?" he heard a young woman asking as they walked by.

Steve didn't know what to make of this gesture. He just smiled and kept on following John. The women were all beautiful to Steve and he got nasty thoughts every time he saw one of his type. Steve kept counting how many of the women he would like to sleep with, checking out the women as he walked by.

Jane also noticed the abundance of women.

"Where are all the men?" she asked, looking around Breitenbush.

"At certain points throughout the town, making sure no one escapes. So, don't have any plans on leaving anytime soon," John said, smiling at Jane.

"Some hunt for us and others do the handy work. The lucky ones get to help us reproduce, Steve, so we can continue our population," Tara said as she gave Steve the sexy eye.

"This is your type of place, Steve. You should join us. Or, maybe not."

"So, you are not gonna kill us?" Steve asked in a nervous tone.

"Haven't decided yet. Plus, I don't know the plans for you." John turned to Steve. His demeanor was friendlier.

"Look. I didn't mean to rough you up so bad, brother. I had to get my revenge licks. Plus, I promised

I wouldn't kill you. Just remember that when the time comes."

"Time for what?" Steve asked as they stopped at an old cabin in the corner of Breitenbush.

John opened the cabin doors. "This is where you will be staying tonight. There is a guard at both exits. So, no need to try and make an escape attempt."

"Are we guests or prisoners?" Steve asked defensively.

"This is our prisoner quarters. Right now, this is where you will stay. We call this place Cabin Fever. If you survive tonight, we will see what tomorrow will bring. There are first aid kits for both of you to clean your wounds and patch up. Sorry for the smell. I haven't had time to remove our old friend," John said with a weird, evil smile.

Steve and Jane entered the cabin and heard John lock the doors behind them. The cabin smelled like death. It was extremely hot like an oven that had been on for days. Sweat ran down the faces of Steve and Jane as they looked into each other's eyes in fear.

"This place is going to kill us. We need to find a way out. And why all of a sudden is John your friend? What the fuck is going on here? What did we get ourselves into? And what is that god awful smell?" Jane kept going.

"Shut the fuck up! Sorry. Let me think." Steve shouted angrily as he paced back and forth in the hot cabin, grabbing his hurt shoulder with blood and body sweat soaking his shirt.

"I don't know what's going on myself. I don't get why this place is named after me. I have questions too." Steve said, holding Jane by the shoulders. Steve looked Jane in her eyes and she looked back in fear.

"I don't wanna die here," Jane said while a tear ran down her cheek, falling off her chin. Steve wiped her tears. Hugged her tightly as the sweat from their bodies stuck to each other.

Jane pushed him away, then looked around again for the source of the smell in the cabin. Her eyes caught a body lying next to a chair on the side of the room.

"Oh my God! It's Rebecca. He killed Rebecca." Steve saw the badly beaten body Jane was referring to and quickly turned away in disgust.

"Who is that?" Steve questioned while trying to cover his nose.

"John's public defender I told you about that hated the guy and made him take the plea deal. This is it. His revenge, Steve. He is going to kill everyone that helped put him away."

Steve hugged Jane for comfort and protection.

"I will not let him kill us. I will fight for you, Jane." Jane pushed him away again out of anger and frustration.

"How could you fall for Tara and this game? I thought you were better than that. You need help. You are sick. I tried to warn you. Whatever happens, this is your fault, Steve."

Steve stood silently to gather his thoughts.

"Let's just play John's game and we shall stay alive long enough to find a way out. We will get through this. I promise I won't leave you here, Jane. I will save you."

Jane grabbed the first-aid kit to clean her thigh and dried-up blood.

"I don't know if I want your help after all. I tried to help you and I'm in this shithole."

Steve grabbed the supplies from Jane and helped her with her wound.

"Saying I'm sorry will never be enough for what I am putting you through. But I promise that I will do

whatever it takes to save you and get you out of here."

As Steve comforted Jane, a small moan was heard in the corner at the opposite end of the cabin. Steve and Jane saw a body that was barely moving. He took Jane by the hand as they moved closer to investigate the body. The corner was dark. The body smelled like urine and feces and death. They could tell it was a woman due to the long beat-up hair as her back was turned to them.

"Hello," Steve whispered to the woman. "Are you OK?" Jane asked.

The woman moaned like a hungry child as she turned around and said, "Help me."

Steve and Jane looked at each other, turned to the woman and yelled in unison, "SAMANTHA!"

12

Jane

As night continued to fall in Cabin Fever, Jane sat in a corner of the cabin after cleaning her wounds. She looked over at Steve lying on his back staring at the ceiling, angry at him for getting her caught up in his mess. She was incensed about his drama and how he had gotten her kidnapped by a crazy psycho like John Dexter. Mad that she fell in love with Steve. Sad that she was used and misled three years ago. Sadder still that her friend, Rebecca, fell victim to John's plot for revenge. Jane shed a small tear for Rebecca as she saw her body slowly decaying in the hot cabin. It was a fate she did not want for herself.

Jane turned her head to look at Samantha. How could she be abusive to her daughter all these years and

I didn't know? She thought to herself as she lay down on the hard floor.

She lay there motionless. Jane closed her eyes and shed another tear as she thought about her own abusive relationship three years ago.

"You sick cheating bastard"! Jane yelled at her husband, Byron.

"What the fuck are you talking about now? You always have some kind of twisted theory in your head," Byron responded as he sat on the sofa drinking his favorite whiskey, watching football—his usual Sunday routine.

Jane handed Byron his phone with a text message from a girl named Terry.

At the sight of his phone being in Jane's hands, he didn't reach for it. Instead, rage flashed in Byron's eyes as his eyebrows sank in. Within a split second, his glass of whiskey was on the floor spilling its contents while he grabbed Jane tightly by the wrist. Jane could see his knuckles become white from how hard he was holding her, but she didn't let the phone go and continued her argument.

"Who is she?" Jane yelled at the top of her lungs while her face was red with rage and pain.

Byron stood up and yelled back at the top of his lungs as his face turned red.

"How many times have I told you to stop going through my fucking phone? She's a client on a case I'm working on."

"Let me go," Jane yelled as she pulled back. "Why does your client want to meet you at three in the morning, Byron?"

"It's a special case I'm working that you weren't a part of. It's confidential," Byron continued to yell at her.

"Even your own wife, Byron? You are always being sneaky and lying to me. Let's see what you are really up to."

Jane dialed Terry's number. As the phone rang, Byron lunged toward Jane to grab his phone.

"Give me my shit back!" Byron yelled as he slammed Jane to the floor.

Terry answered the phone.

"Hey, baby!" Terry answered in a soft, sexy voice. "Hi, Terry. It's Jane. His wife. Here's Byron for you. We're done. Good luck."

Byron snatched the phone from Jane, hung up the call and smacked Jane as hard as he could. He beat her that night, as he had many others. Jane finally had enough of the abuse and ran away to White Pine looking for an escape. An escape that led her to her first big case three years ago to put away John Dexter.

J ane opened her eyes and wiped away her tears from the awful memories that led to her divorce.

If I only knew about Tara, I could have saved her, she thought to herself. She felt Tara's pain.

If I only knew, Jane repeated slowly as she cried herself to sleep.

13

Steve

Steve sat in the opposite corner away from Jane and purposely turned his back away from her to hide his face. The smell of Rebecca's decaying body made him sick to his stomach. Steve wanted to hide his guilt. He felt overwhelmed by his confusion about the events that happened over the last three days, and by the pain he caused Jane and the situation he put her in. His ego was hurt from being used by Tara in her trap.

Steve sat there wanting to be strong but, at the same time, felt defeated. The pain in his chest was more than the bullet wound in his shoulder. If only he hadn't been on that run that day. If only he hadn't been looking for his father. He wouldn't have been in the situation he found himself in now.

Steve sat in the corner thinking about what Tara said, the abuse that Samantha put Tara through when she was younger. He started to remember his own abuse and why he started to run.

S teve woke up to the sounds of shattered glass and a violent scream. It was his mom's boyfriend, who he had always hated. It wasn't unusual for his mother to be fighting with her drunk boyfriend. Steve knew this man was no different. Steve jumped up from his bed and ran as fast as he could to the dining room, where his mom was shaking like a beaten animal. Her hair was tangled and her face was red with a small tear in her eye. A broken glass sat by her feet with blood dripping from her leg.

"I'm sorry, Spencer," Steve's mom said in a soft tone. Spencer was standing very close to Steve's mom with his fist clenched. Grabbing her with a death look in his eyes.

Steve continued his stride and pushed Spencer back as hard as he could.

"Stop! You're hurting her!" He yelled.

Spencer still stood there angry. He held Steve's mother's hand in a threatening grip.

"Let her go! You're hurting her," Steve yelled again.

This time, Spencer struck Steve, sending him to the floor with his mouth dripping in blood. This was the first time Steve was hit while defending his mother. Steve knew he had to be brave.

Spencer looked over at Steve on the floor beginning to tear up.

"I'm just having an adult conversation with your mother, Steve. Go back to your fucking room and go to bed."

Steve slowly got up to his feet and made eye contact with his mother as she wiped her tears.

"It's OK, Steve. It's OK," His mother said.

Steve knew it wasn't. This wasn't the first time Spencer had had too much to drink, but Steve wanted it to be the last.

He rushed Spencer as fast as he could and pushed him, sending him flying across the room. Spencer hit his head on the dining room table on his way down and lay motionless.

Steve's heart jumped out of his chest. Pounding like a drummer gone wild.

"Is he. . . Is he dead?" Steve looked at his mother frantically.

"What did you do? What did you do?"

"I-I don't know." Steve replied, standing in shock.

Spencer let out a small groan as he started to regain consciousness.

Steve's mother grabbed his coat.

"You need to go. Get out! I will take care of this. I will say he got drunk and fell, but you shouldn't be here. Go!"

This broke Steve's heart. His own mother once again taking the side of a no-good boyfriend.

"What about me?" Steve yelled. "What about me?" His mom stood there motionless.

"Until you can put food on the table, it will never be just about you."

Steve shed a tear and ran out the door.

He ran until his legs were sore. He stopped and thought about what his mom had said. Then he ran again. He was thirteen.

Alone, abandoned, and afraid. Steve ran all the way to White Pine looking for his real father but never found him. Instead, Steve found hopelessness and the search for answers in an empty heart. Then Steve returned home and the same story played out there for the next five years.

Steve opened his eyes and wiped away his tears from the awful memories.

If I only knew about Tara, I could have saved her,

he thought to himself. He felt Tara's pain from his own abusive relationship.

If I only knew, Steve repeated slowly as he cried himself to sleep.

14

John Dexter

John Dexter's childhood was a troubled one. He barely knew his father, who had been sent to life in prison for crimes of sex trafficking, murder, and money laundering. John's dad was the leader of a cult inspired by Jim Jones. The same cult he inspired to lead someday and take over the sex world. He longed to be a king in this world.

John's world was crushed when he found out the truth about his family. His mother that he loved so much turned out to be his sister. She named him John because she considered his father another trick in the sex game. A reminder of the deadbeat of a man that impregnated her. A married man that wanted a thrill with a woman that wasn't his wife. She gave birth to a bastard and named him John for a memory of her dark path.

His stepfather physically abused him and sent him to school with black eyes multiple times, eventually leading him to foster care. In family after family, John was rejected or physically harmed—never finding the love he was looking for. The only love he found was from women he abused, and he never wanted to love them back.

Finding the love he wanted led him down a dark path. Falling into the rough crowd led him to his criminal record and multiple stints in county jail. It was there in county jail that John was helpless and gained his desire for power.

"Shower time, boys!" yelled a guard as John lay in his bunk staring at the ceiling. This was John's usual routine since being locked up for his stupid mistakes. Thoughts of what could've been different kept playing in his mind.

The hardest thing about being locked up for John was shower time. Moments he took for granted on the outside and never wanted to do on the inside. This particular day was no different.

John slowly stood up from his top bunk. His room-mate had already gone to the yard to do his daily hustle.

John exited his cell to begin a long walk through a hallway with his shampoo. The hallway was even hotter than his jail cell. John started to sweat. The noise coming out of the units was loud and obnoxious. Inmates yelling and slamming dominoes. Arguing over commissary and what to watch on the television. Minor chatter among the inmates. Yelling over who's going to prison for their crimes. What to do for defense in court. Everyone turns into a lawyer in jail.

John continued to slowly walk through the shower walls as other inmates gave him dirty stares. The cold water echoing through the stalls started to send chills through John's body; he was wearing only boxers and shower shoes. John let the last two inmates cut in front of him, still feeling uncomfortable showering with a bunch of men in jail.

As John got closer and closer to the stalls, he heard and saw Officer Tanya Brown, an overweight female guard, giving stern orders to the men.

"One towel, one soap, one towel, one soap!" shouted Officer Brown.

Closer and closer, John eased his way to the shower room.

John was finally face to face with the female guard as she shoved a tan eleven-inch-wide bath towel and a thin piece of green soap into John's hands. He was then shoved into the humidity of the showers.

The smell of sweat and feces was too much for John to bear as he gagged on his own saliva, trying to hold his breath. John walked swiftly to find an open stall at the end of the shower away from the crowd. Most of the inmates had already handled their business. Exactly what John was hoping for at this time of the shower rotation—an empty shower room.

John finally discarded his boxers while making his way to the showerhead, turned on the barely hot water and let the stream roll down his back. As John looked down at his feet, he saw the gutter was clogged; leftover soap mashed into the floor, boxers, and other crap was floating around in the water, including someone's teeth with fresh blood going down the drain.

"Hi, handsome," he heard as a female smacked his rear side. It was Officer Brown again. She pushed him back with her baton and proceeded to play with his body.

"Don't say a word," Officer Brown told him as she continued to play with his joystick and he got stiffer.

Officer Brown went down on him and John just

stood there, hopeless, not knowing how to react to this sudden encounter.

John tried to step back from Officer Brown, but the guard grabbed his thighs and shoved him deeper in her throat.

As John stood there, the shower running down his back, he was conflicted on how to react. Here he was getting free sexual pleasure but not from a woman he felt attracted to. He actually felt used for the first time.

"What, you don't want it?" Officer Brown asked him as she stood up to look in his eyes.

John tried to clear his throat, thinking of what to say. Knowing that saying the wrong thing may end with him in solitary confinement out of retaliation.

Officer Brown pushed John against the wall and began to unbutton her pants.

"I'm in control now, inmate," Officer Brown whispered in his ear aggressively as she bit down on his ear lobe. Officer Brown forced herself on John. He hadn't been with a woman in months, but this wasn't the woman he wanted. He was being used for Officer Brown's pleasure, but his nightmare got worse.

Officer Brown pulled herself away from John after feeling he was about to explode his internal juices. She took her handcuffs and cuffed John to the showerhead. Officer Brown whistled secretly and another female guard approached John from behind. This time, it was Officer Cleo Ryder

"What—What is this?" John asked, now fearing this may get out of hand. Officer Ryder was a female but had a man's body and clearly wasn't John's type, or any other man's for that matter.

As John stood naked, hopeless and nervous, he could feel Officer Ryder placing her hand on his head and slowly moving down his back, finally reaching his anus. Officer Ryder spat in her hand and lubed John's ass, inserting several fingers into him.

"Please stop!" John begged the guards. Officer Ryder swiped her baton at the back of John's knees, making him fall to the ground.

"Shut the fuck up!" Officer Ryder yelled at John. "I'm in control now, inmate."

"Help!" John yelled at the top of his lungs, but Officer Brown put a dirty bar of soap in his mouth. Then Officer Ryder took her baton and shoved it up his rectum as hard as she could, multiple times, and seemed to be getting pleasure from seeing John in pain. After several minutes of being victimized, he passed out.

Back at his own cabin deep in White Pine, John got angrier as those memories of jail kept playing in his mind. They were the reason for his PTSD and his hatred for women. The reason he would never have respect for women and one day would control them all.

Except for Tara, for some reason. He couldn't explain his love for Tara. His love for power was deeper, and his passion to never let another woman take advantage of him was even deeper still. Only Tara knew about his abuse when he was a young man in jail. That was the reason for their instant connection. They vowed to each other to never again be the victims but the abusers.

John still didn't know how Tara changed his heart. He figured that if he treated her good, she would always be good and loyal to him. John was fascinated by Bonnie and Clyde and wanted his own female partner in crime. After his accused kidnapping of Tara, before his arrest, John and Tara had their fair share of wrongdoings outside of White Pine. It was all going well until Steve went to the police and ruined his freedom and his quest for power.

While John sat in prison, away from Tara, isolated from the world, all he heard was how Steve was a hero. Seeing Steve in his trial gave him nightmares for three years while he was behind bars. It was when John saw

Steve on the news that he decided to plan his escape to seek his revenge. Steve, Jane, the guards, and Breitenbush would all feel his wrath when he killed them one by one until he was the only one standing. This became his mission. That day, we swore he would get his revenge.

As John sat on his sofa looking at Tara sleeping, his past kept replaying over and over in his mind. A past he wanted to change but couldn't escape. John knew this was his time for money, power, and respect. He kept thinking of ways to execute his mission now that he had all the pieces together

"Never lose control. If they only knew." He quietly said to himself. "If they only knew."

As John began to close his eyes and rest his head, Kurt, his most loyal soldier, walked into the cabin to speak with him.

"Boss, big boss ain't happy on how you brought in Steve. He's super pissed right now," Kurt said as he took a seat in front of John.

"I'm the fucking boss now!" John shouted as he stood up to look Kurt straight in his eyes. John pounded on the table in frustration.

Tara rolled over after hearing John's emotions from the other side of the room. She walked over to join John and Kurt's conversation.

"What's going on?" Tara asked while taking a seat next to John.

"Steve! That's what's going on. I'm tired of this so-called hero. Your hero, that is. It's time for him to go," John told the two as he began to light a cigar.

"Well, how do you plan on doing this?" Kurt asked John while lighting his own cigar.

"You should have, I mean, we should have killed him when we had the chance," Tara yelled at John.

"I told you why we couldn't kill them, but this is our chance now. No, this is my chance now. It will all play itself out," John said in between puffs of his cigar. "Well, it sounds easier said than done since he was specially requested by The Man," Kurt responded. "What are you going to with his lady friend? The DA chick?" Kurt asked.

"Leave Jane to me. I'm going to skin her from head to toe and watch her bleed out." Tara jumped in while taking out the knife that was given to her by John as a gift before he went to prison.

John smiled at the enthusiasm of Tara taking on his traits. The room went silent as the three of them thought of ways to get rid of Steve. John had been fascinated with the game of chess since learning it in jail. He always kept a chessboard on his desk to remind him of his life. Chess to John resembled the obstacles of his life. He needed to stay one step ahead of his competition.

John eased up from his seat to grab a drink of whiskey from his minibar. He took a few sips as he stared at his chessboard.

"You know, chess is simple. You take out the king and the pawns will follow. All we have to do is take out the king." John finished his thought and took a seat while taking another puff of his cigar.

"Well, again, how do you suppose we do that without causing too much attention to us?" Kurt asked John, paying close attention to his chessboard.

John, who had been slouched in his chair, slowly fixed his posture.

"Kurt, didn't you do some bomb duty in the army or something back in the day?" John asked as he looked Kurt in his eyes with much intrigue.

"Well, something like that. More like defusing them for combat."

"Well, can you make one or not?"

"Yeah, I think I still have it in me. It's been a while, but hey, we have internet for that now also," Kurt answered as he sat back in his chair to gather his next thought.

"How are we going to get access to the money?" Tara asked.

"Don't worry about that. I have it all figured out with Senator Alan. We're going to use part of the 50 million to get him into the White House. Then he will be my puppet and I will own him. We will use Kurt's bomb and take out the king. I will take place as leader and get the other pawns in line.

"Once Alan becomes President Smith, I will create a pipeline to stream government money back to us in off-shore accounts to create an empire. Whoever gets in my way is dead to me. One thing is for certain. Steve will not make it out of here alive. For him, this is game over," John said.

Kurt moved a piece on the chessboard as John sat back and waited. John took a puff of his cigar and grinned evilly, then yelled, "CHECKMATE!"

15

Surprise Guest

"Ⅱll right, all right, everyone. Gather around."
Sergeant Tim stood at the podium to give a brief press conference to the citizens of White Pine.

"Three days ago, at approximately 6 p.m., someone called in to report a suspicious vehicle illegally parked and a truck that was still running halfway in the street. When White Pine PD arrived on the scene, a body was found in the truck, and the SUV was discovered to belong to DA Jane Goodwright. Currently, the where-abouts of DA Jane are unknown. The Pembleton camera spotted escaped convict, John Dexter, near the truck and SUV. At this time, the whereabouts of John Dexter are also unknown." Sergeant Tim paused to look at the room of reporters as he gathered his thoughts.

"Sergeant, Max Sinclair, from White Pine News. Is it true many people involved in the case of Tara Murphy are also missing at this time, and when did John Dexter escape?"

"I can't confirm the location of others involved in the three-year-old case. All I can confirm is DA Jane is missing and we are working diligently to locate her. As for John, he has been missing for three weeks now. The fugitive task force are tracking him as we speak."

"Sergeant, Jim Gold, from Inside Edition. How close are you to finding John Dexter, and is that a priority?"

"The search for John is not on White Pine's PD radar. His search will be conducted by the FBI and the United States Marshalls. Just because the SUV of DA Jane was found in White Pine doesn't mean she is in White Pine. She may have had some car trouble, got help, and moved on. However, we will search as much of the Adirondacks as we can to either find clues or any answers that may be there. When the time comes, I will update the press if necessary information comes forward. I would like the citizens of White Pine to call us if they see or hear anything out of the ordinary and especially if they see John Dexter. He is to be considered armed and dangerous. Thank you.

Sergeant Tim stepped away from the podium as many reporters shouted his name, wanting to get a question in.

Steve opened his eyes after a short night's sleep in the burning cabin. His body still sore from the miles he walked in the Adirondack mountains and his shoulder still hurting from the bullet John shot in him. Steve just lay there, not wanting to get up but wanting to think about what he got himself into. What if he didn't go to the police? Did he really rescue Tara? Why didn't Tara say Samantha was abusive in the trial? Why did John and Tara go through so much trouble kidnapping him to bring him to a place that is named after him? So many questions ran through Steve's mind as he sat there trying not to tear up. The pain and the hurt were still too much to bear.

Steve realized he needed to be there for Jane and, at the same time, he wanted to confront Samantha. Wanting to know if the story was true. Obviously, she was kidnapped for a reason. But so was he.

Steve sat up from the hard floor and rubbed his

shoulder. "Man, this shit hurts," Steve told himself out loud as he looked around to find Jane, trying to focus his eyes in the dim cabin. The smell from Rebecca's body made Steve cover his mouth with his shirt in an attempt to mask the horrible odor.

"Jane!" Steve looked from corner to corner, but he couldn't see Jane or Samantha.

"Jane!" Steve yelled out again. He jumped to his feet and rushed over to the door to find himself locked inside the hot cabin all by himself.

Steve started banging on the cabin's wood doors as hard as he could in his weak state. Sweat running down his face. Heart racing, jumping out of his chest. He fell to his knees.

"Open up. Let me out of here!" Steve yelled as he kept on pounding away at the door as hard as he could.

The door opened, and a beautiful woman walked in. Steve backed up not knowing what to do or say.

"You must be Steve," the woman said to him, placing some clothes on his chest.

"Uh, who are you and where is Jane?"

"I'm Morgan. One of the housemaids here in Breitenbush. You need to shower and put these close on so you can meet him."

"Meet who?" Steve questioned as he put the clothes down.

Morgan looked at him in admiration. "You are very handsome. We should get acquainted someday." Then she smiled and walked out the door.

Acquainted? Steve thought to himself as he watched Morgan walk away and lock him in the cabin again. "Wait, where are you going? What am I supposed to do?" Steve asked before he couldn't see her anymore.

"Wash up and get dressed. Thirty minutes," he heard her say as she walked away.

The shower didn't work in the cabin—Steve thought it was on purpose because it was a prisoners' cabin. He took the washcloth and managed to get some water out of the broken sink that just dripped water from the faucet. As Steve finished getting dressed, a man walked in. A familiar face to Steve, but he didn't recognize him at first.

"Are you ready to meet our leader?" the man asked Steve while showing him the front door.

"I'm as ready as I will ever be to see this so-called leader of yours. I still have questions," Steve replied as he tried to focus on the man's face.

"What can I do for ya?" the man asked.

"Deputy Johnson?" Steve questioned with a confused look on his face.

The man gave Steve a grin as they walked out the

door together.

"I have been a Breitenite for a long time. Being a Breitenite helps me fill that void. Our leader makes this place wonderful and me being a cop keeps this place off the radar. By the way, my name's Alvin here."

"Even though there is a wanted man like John here and still kidnapping people like Jane and me?" Steve asked, defensively.

"John does what John wants to do." Alvin stopped to pick apples off a tree. "Mmm. My favorite," he said as he took a big bite and handed one to Steve to sample. To Steve's surprise, the apple was one of the best-tasting ever. "Good, right?" Alvin smiled as he continued to devour his apple.

Steve chewed quietly, trying not to look too hungry even though it had been days since his last meal.

The two continued to walk through the garden. Steve noticed the farm animals and the lifestyle of this unusual community. The women dressed provocatively as they danced around the community. Steve was curious and aroused seeing all the half-naked women. As they walked around the Breitenbush colony, Steve noticed two women tied up in a cage. One appeared to be dead.

"Who are they and what have they done?" Steve asked, feeling sorry for the women.

"No one really knows what they have done, but John calls them his pets. That's Cleo, the half-dead one. And the fat one is Tanya. No one is to mess with them, or John gets pissed," Alvin told Steve as they kept walking.

"What's the baton for?" Steve asked while pointing to a baton next to the cage.

Alvin smiled mischievously. "You don't wanna know, trust me."

"What's up with all the other women here?" Steve asked in a soft tone. Wanting to change the focus off the caged women. His mind just couldn't help but wonder about the fantasies and possibilities.

"That's how it works here. This is how we bring in the money to this village. Amongst other things, of course. Even though we don't really need money here. This place has everything you want in life, Steve. Women, booze, food, freedom, no taxes, no assholes or bullshit. Well, we do have John, but. This is the way life was meant to be for guys like you and me. We have very intelligent, attractive, and skilled people here in the colony. Know what? Let me show you the cam rooms."

As the two walked towards another cabin, a gorgeous woman ran up to Alvin and stopped right in front of him.

"Hey, Al, will I see you tonight?" she asked as she gave him a kiss.

"Sure thing, wouldn't miss it for anything, baby!" Alvin said as he kissed her and firmly placed his hands on her ass.

The two wrapped up their kiss, and she was on her way.

"Who was that?" Steve asked, trying not to stare at her ass as she walked away.

"Just my bang of the month," Alvin smiled, knowing that Steve wouldn't get what he was talking about. Steve gave him a confused stare. Alvin pulled out a marijuana joint and began to light it.

"I don't do committed relationships, bro. That shit is for losers. I mean, why should I when you got all this ass right here, man? That's what I do. I bang 'em, then bounce. Smash and dash. I'm telling you this is the life, man." Alvin offered Steve the marijuana, but Steve put his hands up to decline.

"Not a smoker, huh?"

"I'm a runner. Smoking just isn't good for the lungs. I may smoke a cigarette here and there for stress."

Alvin continued the walk to the cabin. It was very well kept on the outside. It was hard to see inside through the windows.

Alvin walked up to the door and looked at Steve with a smile.

"Welcome to booty heaven!" Alvin said enthusiastically like a kid getting his favorite candy. "After you, sir." Alvin held the door open like a bellhop with his arm extended.

Steve walked in to the sounds of passionate pleasure. The atmosphere seemed like a porn studio. Women playing with themselves in front of computers. Some had erotic toys and it aroused Steve.

"You like what you see, don't you?" Alvin asked Steve as he rubbed his own crotch.

"What, what is this?" Steve asked in shock. Feeling both curious and horny, seeing beautiful women enjoying themselves.

"This is how we make the money here. The girls perform cam shows, and the profits go to the community. The best part. We get to go wild and party with the girls these guys fantasize about. We have our own porn site that generates millions thanks to these girls."

"Why are they doing this?" Steve asked, trying not to be too aroused.

"What happens in the woods, stays in the woods. The truth. The lies. These are parts of the lies behind the woods."

Steve stood, frozen, staring at the women once

more. "I still can't believe this is all here. Deep in the woods. How long you guys been doing this?"

"We should get going. They are expecting you for brunch," Alvin told Steve as he closed the door behind them.

Alvin walked Steve to the biggest cabin in the middle of the woods, which reminded Steve of a castle in medieval times but more modern for today's society.

"I can't believe this is all here. It must have taken years to complete this." Steve was still shocked by how beautiful the place looked among the trees. A real-life garden of fantasy. A sign posted in the middle called it the Garden of Breitenbush.

"Our leader is a smart guy. That's why we follow him. I mean, for myself, I guess. We keep this place off the radar. I should say, I keep this place off the radar. My job in law enforcement is to make sure this place is never found. It is a big risk if we get spotted. I kind of hate doing this sometimes, man. Being a man of the law but a victim of sexual pleasure. I'm addicted, bro. Addicted to beautiful women and sex," Alvin said while putting out his marijuana blunt and opening the doors to the cabin.

"Welcome home, Steve," Alvin told him as he escorted Steve through the front door.

"I'm not sure what you mean by home. I am still

here against my will. You guys kidnapped me, remember?"

"It will all make sense in just a few minutes. Follow me."

Steve followed Alvin through the kitchen and into a big dining hall where he spotted Jane, who was sitting at a table in a row full of women. The women sat on one side and the men sat on the other. At the head of the table sat a man very recognizable to Steve, but he couldn't figure out who the man was. He had a beard that made him look like he hadn't shaved in years. Like he had been deserted on an island. Like he wanted to resemble Jesus in a long white robe.

The man saw Steve and immediately got up and ran towards him, giving him a big hug.

Steve made eye contact with Jane and gave her a blank stare.

The man looked into Steve's eyes. "It's nice to see you again, son."

Steve pushed back and looked the man up and down. "Dad?"

16

Family Reunion

"Hello, son. Nice to finally see you again and welcome to your new home. Man, you have grown so much. I can't believe you are here now."

Steve just stood there staring at a man he hadn't seen in years. A man he thought was dead. A man that deserted him. The reason for Steve's pain. The man he had been searching for after his mother's boyfriend had beat him. His father was alive and well, living in White Pine. Looking healthier than he had thought.

"Dad, wha—what are you doing here? What happened to you all these years?" Steve was trying not to sound like a desperate boy missing his father in front of the people around the breakfast table.

"I have been watching from a distance, Steve. I

never left you like you thought. I know you have so many questions, son. But we should eat for now and we can catch up later as you get more settled in."

As Steve's father placed an arm around his son, John rose from the table. "Excuse me, sir David, I have some inventory to count."

"That's fine, Sir John. Carry on. And get those women in those cages some food." David turned to Steve again.

"Shall we?"

"**Y**ou need to get your shit together, Kurt."

"Fuck you, Alan. Or should I say, Senator. I know what I'm doing."

John walked in on the two men arguing.

"Shut the fuck up already. We need to get this shit done so we can move on with our plan. I need you, Senator Alan, to go back to the district and listen to the police scanners, and Alvin stays here with me. Kurt, continue to work on the bomb and we will take care of our fearless leader and his bitch boy."

Alvin walked in with Tara. "Sorry we're late. It was hard to sneak from the table with Steve's loyal guards around." Alvin announced his entrance.

John turned to them both as he lit a cigarette. "Don't forget we have $50 million on the line and the village is ours. The White House is ours. This plan must work flawlessly. Don't fuck this up, Alvin. Don't get high before we execute."

"All right, all right! I hear you, man. Let's run through the plan one more time."

John put out his cigarette and looked around the room at his loyal team looking back at him.

"Gather around and listen up, everybody."

"I'm so happy you're here, son. It's been a while since I've seen your face."

"More like twenty-five years. Is that long enough for you?" Steve snapped back quickly.

"I know I have a lot of explaining to do. I will tell you everything when the time is right, but I need you here now. I know it may seem like I'm asking a lot for being out of your life. But . . ."

David paused as he gathered his next thoughts. "You have to trust me, son. You will like it here.

Let us just finish our breakfast and head to my chambers. Everything will come into light then and you will see. Trust me."

Steve looked around at all the faces sitting at the dinner table. His eyes locked onto Jane. They sat there and stared at each other. Jane managed to crack a smile and waved at Steve. She looked beautiful and he wanted to hug her and say sorry for the mess he put her in.

Steve's eyes rolled back to his plate. Then back at Jane.

I'm going to get out of here, even if it means killing my father, Steve thought to himself as he looked at his long-lost father.

182

17

The Truth

It was the most awkward breakfast Steve could remember in his adult life. His father continued to smile at him as if they were at some bizarre annual family get-together. He didn't appear regretful that he hadn't been there for Steve for most of his life, or even acknowledge the fact. Steve wanted answers but didn't know how to feel that he had finally found his father.

This explained things, though. It explained why his father had abandoned him and his mother twenty-five years ago. He'd decided to lead an underground cult. A sex-crazed, male-dominant cult. Steve's face warmed when he thought of all the tantalizing females just outside the door. Like father, like son, he supposed. His thoughts got the best of him when he realized his father chose the cult over him. The women and freedom over being a father to a son in need.

Steve gripped his fork tightly, shoveling eggs and biscuits into his mouth, but they had lost their appeal. Steve was hungry from not having a full meal the last three days but seeing his father all of a sudden made him lose his appetite.

And Jane . . . Steve wasn't sure if Jane was keeping up appearances or if she really was enjoying breakfast with these crazy sick-os. Steve wanted to know Jane's thoughts and wanted to escape with her.

David spoke and joked with many of the men he hosted at his breakfast table, talking about his favorite women in the village, sexual fantasies, and how they should invest in top-notch filming equipment for their internet business. The men and women treated David like a king and respected him like he was royalty. He was their leader and the man they admired. Steve hated that David was being idolized and all he wanted was a father to be in his life.

"Have you thought about being in front of a camera, Jane?" David asked with a sly grin.

Jane must have been faking her earlier smile. Now her lips were pressed tightly together, her face pale. She looked like she might vomit in her mouth. Steve could tell this really bothered Jane and it wasn't her type of party.

"No, not my thing," She finally replied after a small pause. Jane didn't even look in David's direction and kept her eyes on the breakfast plate.

Steve couldn't hold his tongue any longer and decided to speak up for Jane. "You kidnap these women," he said. "You kidnap them and bring them here and brainwash them so you can pleasure yourself whenever you want? You put our last name on it like it's part of me too. How could you do this to them?" Steve slammed his fork down, waiting for a response. The table went quiet and everyone looked at Steve with appalled faces. David raised his grey eyebrows. "It's not brainwashing, son," he said. "We called it enlighten-ment. Everyone benefits for the colony around here and, most importantly, no government to tell us what to do or take money from us," David said in an authorita-tive tone.

The table applauded and agreed with David. "Oh, God," Jane groaned from the other end of the table. Every male eye turned to her in disgust. She focused on her plate, pushing food around. Not wanting to look up but felt the eyes on her.

David wiped at his mouth with a napkin and glanced at Steve's plate. "You finished, son?"

Steve nodded mutely. He was finished with this nightmare. This unexpected reunion with his father. This was not the family reunion Steve thought he would have.

Questions plagued Steve's mind. He wanted to scream at his father, shake him until his bones rattled. Not just for what he did to him and his mother . . . but for what he was doing to all these women. Steve wanted to save them, and he thought it was the right thing to do. Be the savior of Breitenbush.

Steve was no saint. He had screwed over plenty of women, but he hadn't done anything like this. He loved women in a cherishing way. Admired them even though he couldn't commit to just one. His obsession was different from John and his father.

David smiled. "Wonderful." He stood. "Walk with me."

Steve caught Jane's eye. "What will you do with Jane?" he demanded.

"Not to worry, Steve," David said, clapping a large hand on his shoulder. Steve winced. "As long as she doesn't give us any trouble, we won't give her any. She'll be in the guest cabins, safe and sound. I promise."

Jane set down her fork, done with her meal. "I'll be fine, Steve," she said stiffly. "Come find me when you're done . . . catching up." She looked David up and down with such loathing, Steve wondered why his father hadn't caught fire.

As Steve and David left the dining room, David leaned in to mutter, "A tight ass, that one. You bone her?"

Steve's skin crawled. "That's none of your business."

"I'll take that as a yes, then."

David led Steve around a beautiful garden tended by women who wore short shorts and pushup bras, their hair tied back in braids. Sweat glistened on their toned bodies like oil. Steve pushed down his arousal. Clearing his mind of his filthy thoughts.

"I apologize about John's aggressive methods of getting you here. He was instructed not to harm you. Even though he holds a grudge against you for putting him away. I will deal with him accordingly." David said. Steve felt his wounded shoulder throb.

"It was so ironic seeing you in the news as the man putting John behind bars. I should have reached out to you sooner, but I wasn't ready to face you, son. I could have stopped the pain for you both but I was not ready to confess to you. A vacation for John was something he needed for doing his own thing outside the community."

"That man is a murderer, an escaped felon, and

who knows what else. You shouldn't be associated with him. He's bad company," Steve said darkly, furious that his father held John to such high standards. "John did what he had to do, does what he wants to do, is who he is," David said. "All that matters is that you're here. Plus…"

David took a deep breath in, then let out a small sigh with his exhale. "He's family, Steve. We protect the family." "Well, he's not my family, and I will turn him in again and again if I have the chance," Steve responded confidently.

David stopped in his tracks to turn to Steve. A long pause of silence hovered over the two of them until David finally started to speak.

"Do you remember Grandpa Matthew? Well, before he was sent to prison years ago, he had one last bang. I guess you can say that. He had a son while he was in jail and now that's John's dad also. Which makes him your uncle. My stepbrother. So, he is family if you like him or not. In fact, Steve, Grandpa ran this village for years and when he was finally caught, he asked me to take over as leader and look after John. I just couldn't get him out of foster care until he left county jail. So, I have been looking after him ever since. Plus," David smirked a little, "Don't you see the resemblance of how we all love women. It's a family trait."

"Are you kidding me? That son of a bitch is my blood?" Steve yelled back at David. "That mother-fucker tried to kill me."

David put his hands up in defense.

"Calm down, son. John had it rough unlike you. He means you no harm. Just a little rough around the edges. All that matters is that you are here now."

"Why did you leave me all alone for this place? I needed you. I have looked for you all these years and you were here all along. Why did you do this to me?" Steve asked, trying not to tear up after getting the courage to ask his father what he wanted to know. "I didn't leave you, son. Your mother and I met here at this colony when your grandfather was in charge. Your mother didn't agree with the policies here and ran off with you in the middle of the night. She told me to never contact you and stay away. I did as she asked but I kept an eye on you as much as I could. It wasn't my idea to leave you. It was your mother's. You have to ask your mother why she kept me away from you. But you are here now and that's important to me," David told Steve in a disappointed tone.

"Why am I here?" Steve demanded.

David reached for a pink rose. He snapped it off its bush, pricking his finger in the process. A droplet of scarlet blood blossomed on his thumb. He didn't seem to mind—he popped his thumb in his mouth and sucked the blood away before gently stroking the petals of the rose as they walked. "Your grandfather created something wonderful here, Steve," he said. "I helped see his dream come forward. But I won't be around forever. I'm getting old—as some of the younger men here are noticing."

He lowered his voice. "I believe they plan to overthrow me as their champion and leader."

Steve felt no sympathy for the man in front of him. He remained silent. David began to pluck the petals from the rose.

"I need an heir," David said. "Someone who understands what I'm doing and embraces it." He stopped walking and looked at Steve square in the eyes. "We're the same blood, you and I. I know you have commitment issues. A quivering desire to claim a woman, to possess her when you'd like and how you'd like. It's in your nature."

David placed a hand on Steve's shoulder. Steve shook him away. "You do not have to fight your nature here, son," David said softly.

Steve stepped up to David, shoving his face inches from his father's. "I don't harm and kidnap women. I won't and I don't want any part of this mess. This is not my life. I'm not you."

"They love it here," David said with a smile. "They're far from abusive families, boyfriends, husbands. The government telling them what to do. They have no responsibilities. They're free. And they take great pleasure in the lifestyle I have made for them here." His eyes wandered as he said this, taking in the form of a young woman bending to trim a plant, her breasts bulging out of her bra.

Steve felt dry in the back of his throat. "This is wrong," he said. "You're a psycho motherfucker. You have women in cages."

David frowned. "From what I hear, those women couldn't keep their hands to themselves in jail. That is John's project that he will take care of when he sees fit. But, son, don't be like that. We can be happy here together, you and me. A family. Don't you want that? We can make good things here. Even get John in line too."

Steve shook his head. "You're too late, Dad," he said. "Twenty-five years too late."

A lvin rolled a joint, leaning against the wall of his cabin, facing the small bomb. Fuck John. He could get his feel-good on before blowing up that self-righteous prick who thought he was a great leader.

David didn't deserve special treatment. Didn't deserve to be a leader of the colony. He shouldn't be the one making all the damn rules. At least, that's what John and Tara always harped on about. Alvin was just tired of David taking all the exotic beauties and using them up before anyone else could have a go at them.

He smiled as he smoked, a rush sweeping through his head. After this, Alvin could take all the exotic ones he wanted.

After feeling doped up enough to shoot through the sky, he picked up the bomb and put it carefully into a duffle bag. He hoisted it on one shoulder, then peeked outside his cabin, taking in the gorgeous scenery of women dancing along the paths and bathing in the lake.

He walked over to David's large luxury cabin, listening for any sound. He knocked on the door. There was no answer.

He was probably teaching his wimpy kid how to properly please a woman, Alvin thought with a small giggle. He could go for a nice, slow lovemaking dance right now. He checked the door. It was unlocked.

Opening the door slowly, he peeked inside,

straining his ears for the sound of anyone in the cabin's entryway. Nothing.

He stepped quietly inside the cabin, getting his bearings. From the looks of it, no one was home.

Alvin let out a sigh, then jumped nearly a foot in the air when his police radio bleeped. "Deputy Johnson, you there?"

Alvin's throat went dry. Sergeant Tim shouldn't be able to reach him all the way out here in the boonies. Not unless . . .

Shit. Alvin cleared his throat and replied, "Here, sir."

"Thank God. I've been trying to reach you." Alvin waited, expectant.

"The feds are on the hunt. I've managed to lead them astray, but they're close. Too close. Whatever you do, don't set off that fucking bomb," Tim told him halfway out of breath.

A sweat broke off on Alvin's forehead. "Yes, sir, I will let John know," he said into the radio. He set down the duffle bag and removed the bomb, staring in panic at the blinking red light. It was a manual bomb, one that would go off when Alvin pressed the button on a remote a safe distance away.

But what if something else triggered it? He couldn't

have a live bomb sitting around waiting for someone to pull the trigger!

He knelt on the ground, fumbling with the wires. The high from the blunt settling in. "Dammit, Alvin,"

he muttered to himself. "Is it the red or blue wire? Red means no, blue means . . . go? No, that's not it." He wiped off the sweat that had gathered on his nose. He wasn't thinking straight. The drugs muddled his brain, making him overconfident that whichever wire he cut, it would be the right one.

I can diffuse this bomb, he thought to himself.

Retrieving a pocketknife from his trousers, Alvin selected the blue wire.

He cut it.

18

The Plan

Steve threw himself onto the ground as an earth-shattering explosion echoed along the hidden valley.

David dove down next to him, slinging an arm around Steve's head protectively. The women in the garden screamed and leaped into the flower beds, shuddering and moaning in fright.

Steve looked up, shaken. "What . . . what happened?" he asked.

David frowned, looking towards a plume of smoke not far from the garden. "My cabin. Someone blew it up."

Steve scrambled to his feet. "Why?" he demanded, his voice shaking.

David slowly hauled himself to his feet, his eyes glittering with malice. "The other men. They want to kill me. After all I've accomplished, all I've done for them. I'll become a martyr yet."

Steve rolled his eyes. His father really was a pompous asshole. "I have to find Jane," he said. "Make sure she's all right."

Steve turned to leave, but David grabbed his arm, yanking him back. "Are you out of your mind, boy?" he demanded. He jabbed a finger in the direction of the explosion. "Someone just tried to kill me! You're in as much danger as I am." He pulled Steve away in the opposite direction, towards the trees. "You have to come with me. I have a safe house no one knows about. It's the only place we'll be safe."

Steve yanked his arm out of his father's grip. "I'm not hiding away with you," he spat. "You're the reason I'm in this mess, and you pulled Jane into it, as well. I'm not going anywhere with you."

David frowned. "You don't know what you're doing, Steve," he said. "Don't sacrifice yourself for one woman. Look." He gestured to the women who had gotten to their feet, pointing towards the smoke and gossiping amongst themselves. "We'll take them with us. I'm basically their savior. Their God. They'll do whatever I ask."

Steve punched his father across the jaw, hard.

David stumbled back, stunned.

"What was that for?" he asked, mystified.

"For everything," Steve growled. "I don't want to see you again, Dad. Ever." Steve realized he made his peace with not having his father in his life after finding him in this disappointing way.

He spun on his heel and sprinted towards the prison cabins, where he knew Jane would be held.

"I have to save Jane," he said to himself. "I have to save Jane."

Sergeant Tim stared in disbelief at the plume of smoke that hovered above the trees, about a mile away. Above Breitenbush.

The FBI agent next to him scowled and radioed in. "You see that?" he asked.

"Moving in now," came the static reply.

"Wait." Sergeant Tim scrambled for a way to save the colony, to salvage the mistake that idiot, Alvin, had committed. "You're going in this blind," he said. "What if there are more bombs? Who set it off? We should assess the situation more carefully. It's not smart."

The federal agent gave him a smirk. "No offense,

Sarg, but this is our rodeo. Don't tell us how to do our jobs."

He walked away, leaving Sergeant Tim frustrated.

Damn that fool Johnson. Why had he set off the bomb after he strictly told him not to?

Now they were all doomed. Pulling out his cell, Sergeant Tim called John Dexter's number.

John picked up on the second ring. "Hey, Sarg."

"John. What the hell happened over there?" Sergeant Tim spat.

"No fucking clue. It looks like Alvin offed himself, the fucking moron."

"Well, you're running out of time. The feds are about a mile away. Grab as many girls as you can and leave."

"Yes, sir."

John hung up and Sergeant Tim pocketed his phone. The feds would call in a chopper. It would be there at any moment. They were in for a shock.

Tara opened the door, stepped inside the cabin, and shut it behind her, ready for a final fight with her mother. It was time for Tara's revenge after all these years.

Samantha shifted in the corner with a groan.

"Tara . . ." she rasped.

Tara marched over to her mother and gave her a swift kick in the ribs. Samantha fell forward, curling in on herself with a high-pitched moan.

"Bitch," Tara spat. "I should have ended this years ago. Now that you're here . . ." She knelt down, grabbed her mother by the root of her dirty blonde hair, and tugged her head back, forcing her to look at her. "Now I can do as I please with you."

Samantha whimpered. "Please, Tara," she said. "I'm sorry. Please forgive me."

Tara laughed, a sharp, chilling sound. "It's too late now for pitiful apologies," she sneered. "You should have never laid a hand on me. Never lied to me. Never sent me to that facility."

"I was wrong," Samantha sobbed. "I should have never treated you the way I did. I'm sorry, Tara. You know I love you."

Tara smacked Samantha across the face. "Don't lie to me!" she shouted. "You never loved me in your life! You did this to me."

"I'm sorry, I'm sorry . . ." Samantha muttered over and over again, defending herself from Tara's attack.

Tara shook her head. "You're pathetic," she said. "Death would be a better fate for you."

Samantha squeaked.

Tara kicked her again and again, sending her flying back into the wall. Slowly, she kneeled, tracing a finger along her mother's terrified face. "I so wanted to love you," Tara whispered.

Tara lowered her hand to Samantha's throat and squeezed.

Samantha brought her boney hands to Tara's, trying to pry it off.

Tara only added her other hand, clamping it on her mother's pale neck. Samantha choked and turned purple, trying to pull in a breath, but none came. She began to kick and twist, but she was so frail, so weak. She no longer had enough energy to fight.

Tara stared into her mother's bulging eyes, taking pleasure in choking the life out of the woman who nearly beat her to death every weekend.

The door burst open and John strode in. Tara growled and released her mother, letting her fall back, gasping for air.

"What the hell are you doing?" John snapped. "You haven't killed her yet? I've been looking for you. Did you hear the bomb go off?"

Tara nodded. "I assumed David was dead. I thought I'd make death a trend today," she said, shooting a look at her mother.

John took Tara by the shoulders and shook her.

"The feds are nearby. That explosion fucking blew our cover. They're on their way now."

Fear soared into Tara's throat. "Fuck," she said. "We have to get out of here."

"Not before killing David and Steve first," John said darkly. "They will get away, David is a master at disappearing. He'll start up somewhere else. We have to take him down. Now or never. I need to end him. Steve needs to get what he deserves for putting me away. You know this."

Tara gritted her teeth. "Why the hell did the bomb go off if David wasn't around?"

"How the fuck do I know?" John exploded. "But he wasn't home when it went off."

"We're too late, then," Tara said bitterly. "He's probably long gone now that he knows someone is trying to kill him."

John rubbed his chin. He scowled at Tara's mother, who lay on the floor, whimpering. "Jane," he said. "That bitch we had to drag along. Steve won't leave without her. We could use him as a bargaining chip and her as bait."

"Please," Tara drawled. "David doesn't really care about Steve."

"We'll see," John said. He pulled her arm, dragging

her out of the cabin. "Let's find Jane. Hopefully she's still in the cabin where we left her."

"And then what?" Tara asked.

John grinned. "Then we wait for Steve."

19

The Fight

Jane heard the explosions and fell to the ground as the cabin shook.

She frantically ran to the door but found it locked. She was trapped again. A prisoner of the sex cult. No way out. Nowhere to turn. No Steve for help.Moments later, she heard footsteps approach the door slowly. Tara slammed the door open. Jane looked up. "What was that explosion?"

"The plan," Tara responded with a smirk, holding the knife John gave her.

"Plan? What plan?" Jane noticed the knife and stepped back.

Tara lunged at Jane. Jane sidestepped the blade as it ripped a piece of flesh from her shoulder.

Tara lost her balance, stumbling into the wall. Jane swiftly jumped on Tara, placing one hand on the blade and the other around her neck.

Jane got the upper hand on Tara when they both fell to the floor. Jane felt something hard and cold in the back of her head. Then a gun cocked.

"Don't move, bitch!"

Steve had barged in on too many couples making love in his search for Jane. Maybe they didn't care that a bomb just went off. Maybe they thought it was the end of the world and said, "Fuck it." He didn't really know nor care.

Jane had to be here somewhere.

He looked through the guest cabins, smashing in the doors or breaking windows to get inside.

"I gotta save Jane. I gotta save Jane," Steve kept repeating as he ran through the compound.

Finally, he kicked in a door and spotted Jane pressed against the wall, eyes wide.

"I'm here, Jane," he said, stepping through the door.

"Steve, stop!" she screamed.

Steve felt something make contact with the back of

his head, and he flew forward, stars exploding in his vision. He managed to catch his fall and spun around.

John and Tara had been waiting for him.

"You know what, Steve?" John drawled, turning a gun on him. "I've decided that you're bad luck." John cracked a smile.

"I wish David had never fucked your whore of a mom," Tara drawled.

"We would have been happier . . . I would have been happier without you."

Steve clenched his fists. "I didn't know about your situation, Tara," he said. "You can't blame me for that. I did the right thing anyway. John is no good and I don't care if he's my uncle."

"Uncle?" Jane questioned, looking confused.

Steve turned to Jane. "It's a long story. I just found out myself."

Tara interrupted the reunion. "But I do," she said, her eyes glittering with hatred. "If you hadn't been on that fucking run . . . if you hadn't reported what you saw to the police . . ."

"You're sick, Tara," Steve said. "My dad, John . . .

they've poisoned your mind. They don't care about you. They only want to use you. I'm sorry."

Tara slapped Steve hard across the face.

"You don't know me," she hissed.

Nothing about her was the strong, sweet girl he had taken in for the weekend. Her gentle touch, her skin sparkling with passion and desire . . . it was all gone.

Steve hated himself for falling for her trap. They got him right where they wanted him. Tara's revenge plot and John's quest for power.

Tara kneed Steve between the legs. He crumpled onto his knees, floored by the pain. Tara punched him again. His lip split and blood started to leak from his mouth.

"You're a piece of shit, Steve," she said, increasing the speed of her punches.

"Get him, cupcake," John purred at the door, relaxing his grip on the gun. "Beat the shit out of him."

"Stop!" Jane cried, jumping on Steve's back to defend him.

"Tara, listen . . ."

Tara threw Jane off Steve. "John, shoot her, will you?" Tara yelled while she continued her attack.

Steve watched as John turned the gun on Jane, cocking it.

"No!" Steve screamed.

The door banged back open. Tara stopped punching Steve. He struggled with consciousness, lifting his head enough so he could see through his swollen eye. David stood in the doorway, arms outstretched.

"John, Tara," David said, voice calm. "Why all this violence?"

Steve's heart jumped. His father had come after him. His father came to rescue him and Jane.

Maybe he wasn't a piece of shit after all. John turned the gun to David.

"Well, look what we have here. Is it my no-good half-brother, Dave? Daddy's favorite son."

David tried to console his brother. "Father loved us both."

"Bullshit," John yelled at David. "He put you in charge of this village. To run the colony. I'm the bastard son. I'm the screw-up, right? He never cared about me when he was in prison and I was getting my ass beat by Grandpa. Where was he when I was in foster care? Where was he? Your damn step-sister should have kept her legs closed. He gave you everything and left me to fend for myself. It was all about David. David, David, David."

John and Tara exchanged glances. Tara drew out her gun.

Without another word, they fired round after round into David, unloading on him.

Steve watched in horror as his father staggered back with each blow, his eyes wide, his shirt soaking through with blood.

As if in slow motion, he fell to the ground, collapsing a dead man.

"Ha!" John danced. Blowing on the top of the barrel like in the wild west. "Got him!"

Tara let out a triumphant cry, leaping into John and wrapping her legs around his waist. "We did it, baby," she said, planting kisses on his face.

As John and Tara celebrated, Steve stared in mute horror at his father, blood pooling around his still body. Jane's hand settled on his shoulder. "I'm so sorry, Steve," she whispered.

Every movement hurt, but Steve crawled to his father's body. He thought he might throw up.

"Dad?"

David didn't respond. He lay face-down, arms splayed out the way they had been when he entered the cabin.

John and Tara's cries of victory were drowned out as Steve crawled his way to his dad, unable to believe he had found him and had him ripped away from him just as quickly.

He touched his father's back and noticed the gun in his back pocket.

He could end this. Here and now.

Steve pulled the gun out of its holster, cocked it, and pointed it at John.

John and Tara froze, then Tara sneered. "Do it," she said. "I dare you."

Steve willed his finger to pull the trigger, to end those two miserable lives. He shook. His vision blurred.

John snorted. "You fucked this wimp?"

"Not my proudest moment," Tara replied. "Come on, Steve, shoot us! Think about how I betrayed you. Think about how I coaxed you into a mind-blowing fuck. You really thought I wanted you. You're dumb as shit."

Her words tore at him, made him quake with anger.

Do it, he told himself. Do it now. But he couldn't. John and Tara laughed, but their merriment was

cut short by the sound of a chopper flying overhead and the sound of a megaphone echoing across the valley. "FBI. Everyone come out of your homes with your hands in the air."

"Fuck," John growled.

"Go," Steve said, his gun still trained on them. "Run while you still can." He knew it was a stupid move not to hold them until the police arrived to arrest them, but he knew he was about to pass out. If he did, he and Jane would be dead. He needed them gone. He needed to save Jane. With his father gone, Steve couldn't risk giving John another notch on his belt as a victim.

Tara leered at Steve as she passed him, following John out the door. "This isn't over yet, Steve," she said. "I'll haunt your dreams. I'll be there in your darkest fantasies. And one day, I'll be there to fuck you over."

He didn't respond.

The moment Tara and John ran out of the cabin, he collapsed, letting himself drift into a dark abyss.

20

The Date

Steve peeled his eyes open, blinking up at the ceiling in his bedroom and silently cursing himself for not getting all the papers graded last night.

Sitting up, he reached for his phone and turned off the alarm. He'd dismissed his earlier alarms, the ones urging him to get up and finally start running again. But he couldn't. Not yet.

Tara had cracked his ribs and given him a mild concussion at Breitenbush a month ago. She had killed his father. Threatened to come after him again. Cursed his existence. If only he hadn't gone on that fucking run.

He wasn't afraid to start running again; he just wasn't ready. It would be painful. It would stir up bad memories. Each night before bed, he said he'd try in the morning, and each morning, he snoozed his alarms, plunging back into a sleepy world of violent nightmares.

It was the weekend. Steve got up, took a warm shower, and picked a crisp button-up from his closet. He stared at himself in the mirror. His face looked significantly better than it did a week ago. It no longer had the purple and green bruises, but it still looked swollen. It was healing.

He walked to the nearby café, hands in his pockets, keeping his eyes on the ground. He checked his watch. He was late.

When he stepped inside the café, he spotted Jane sitting at a table against the window. She waved him over with a smile when she saw him. He wearily sat down across from her. "Hey," he said.

"Hey. How're you feeling today?"

He shrugged. "I'm not as sore as usual. Should be good as new in another week."

Jane nodded. "Good."

Steve looked over at the crutches leaning against the window. "How's physical therapy?"

"A bitch," she said, sipping on a coffee. "But I won't need those in a few weeks. I was lucky my leg didn't get infected."

Steve nodded solemnly. "So, no word on Tara and John?"

Jane shook her head. "They've disappeared. We have no leads. But I'm joining the FBI task force in hunting them down, Steve. We are going to get them for what they did to your father. I am taking the fight to them. I am going to get them. I promise. It's a new hunt."

Steve gritted his teeth. "Maybe if I had just found courage back at that cabin . . ."

Jane placed a hand over his. "Steve," she said quietly. "You did the right thing."

He set his jaw.

Jane leaned back in her seat. "The victims of the cult have been returned home to their families, most of them. Some of them are still in shelters. They're getting the help they need. We did the right thing in a difficult circumstance. We saved them. You are a hero again."

"And Samantha?" Steve questioned

"She's traumatized and severely malnourished, but she'll survive. She will need mental help after all of this. Very lucky Tara didn't kill her also. For everything she put Tara through."

Steve nodded. "Good." The waitress came by and he ordered a coffee. "And the Breitenites?" he asked.

"As many as we could round up? Standing trial.

Including Sergeant Tim. I still can't believe no one saw through his lies and misleads all this time. He really fooled us. We actually found out he joined after John was in jail from the trail and he was the one to help John escape the work detail. Tim and Alvin covered it up. There were many lies, Steve. Many lies behind the woods."

Steve shook his head. "I still can't believe . . . this whole time . . ."

"I know," Jane said softly. "I know." She watched Steve carefully. "But we can trust each other, Steve. We're not alone in this."

Steve's eyes met hers. He felt a surge of attraction to her, one that went above physical beauty. "I never said sorry for putting you through what I put you through. So, I'm sorry. But also, thank you for coming to warn me about John. I appreciate that. Do you want to grab dinner sometime?" Steve finally asked after his apology.

She smiled. "I'd like that. And you are welcome. The apologies are not needed. I think moving forward and putting them both behind bars is what we need for closure."

"I agree," Steve said as his coffee arrived. "So, it's a date."

Jane smiled while she took a sip of her own coffee.

Steve's phone buzzed in his pocket. He reached for it and noticed a text from an unknown number. Steve read it to himself as the room went silent around him:

"I'm always watching you," the message read.

Steve knew it was Tara or John trying to get in his head. It wasn't the first message he had received since escaping his hell a month ago, but he didn't want to involve Jane.

Jane and Steve spent about an hour in the café before the conversation went quiet. The TV in the café had a breaking news report saying Senator Alan was ahead in the polls to be the next United States President.

"I think we should go. I need to finally grade some papers."

"Good idea. I have physical therapy today and it's a long drive back," Jane said as she grabbed her purse.

The two walked outside as Steve held the door open for Jane.

"Where did you park? I'll walk you to the car," Steve said as he grabbed her hand.

"It's OK, don't worry about it. I'm just right there." Jane pointed to her car and let the doors unlock with her key fob.

Steve watched Jane walk to her car and get inside.

Again, another text message buzzed Steve's phone in his pocket.

"You're next, bitch. I'm in control now."

BOOM!

Steve fell as Jane's car blew when she tried to start her ignition. The ground shook, blowing out the windows of the café they just left. Screams were heard throughout the air. Smoke and fire filled the space where Jane once sat.

"Jane! Jane!" Steve yelled as he frantically ran to her car.

The flames were too hot for Steve to try to save her.

No sign of Jane's existence.

Steve fell to his knees in defeat. All he could do was stare. Stare at the flames that once were a car. The only person that knew what he went through was gone at the hands of John Dexter.

It was at that moment Steve knew it was time to be the hunter and not the prey. It was time to take the fight and the hunt back to his uncle. John Dexter himself. Finish Jane's mission for justice for his father.

It was time for the hunt behind the woods.

21

Epilogue: Tara

I t had been a year since Tara's release from a mental institution for her bipolar depression. The illness was diagnosed by her mother for blaming the abuse marks on Tara's face. Even the community of White Pine thought it was Munchausen syndrome by proxy. Tara was forced to have therapy sessions with a psychiatrist. She was wrongfully placed at Pine County Rehab by her psychiatrist, who tried to force himself on her during one of their sessions. When Tara defended herself, he injected her with Propofol to put her to sleep and placed her on a psychiatric hold to cover his wrongdoings.

Samantha tried to get her out, but Tara refused to take her medication in an act of rebellion. Months went by that caused terror for Tara. Not only was she abused at home, but she was bullied in the facility as well for being a gorgeous-looking girl in an out-of-place situation. The woman personally withheld her belongings and refused to give her basic hygiene items so she could watch Tara cry and suffer. The male personnel always tried to make sexual advancements towards Tara, knowing that no one would believe the bipolar girl. This crushed Tara but also made her stronger.

Tara had to continue to fight the other patients after taking too much bullying and name-calling for her pretty looks. Oftentimes, it was she that got the punishment even though it didn't start with her. After each fight, she had to sit with a counselor to discuss her problems. It was during a counseling session that the counselor suggested that she should use her looks for good. Tara realized she could be a model and an activist for others that suffered from bullying.

She started to comply with the rules of the facility and appear to take her medication, but to only trade it for food on days the mental health aides didn't feed her. Joint counseling with her mother, Samantha, helped her get released back to her mother's care. That was a year ago.

Tara opened her eyes from the nightmare that sent her back to her abusive mother. The abuse continued but the help for Tara stopped. She lay there, motionless, as those events at Pine County Rehab gave her the strength to move one.

"If they only knew," Tara said to herself. "If they only knew."

It is early morning breakfast at the Murphy home. Samantha is cooking Tara's favorite sausage omelette, excited to fill out college applications. Samantha is so excited to see her only daughter get a head start in life. For Samantha, college is the only way.

"Tara, come eat your breakfast. We have a busy day looking at colleges for you. I think we should look at one of the Florida colleges since you like the beach climate so much."

Tara slowly walks in with her phone in her hand as it never leaves her eyes.

"Can we do it tomorrow? It's the weekend. I don't have any options for college right now," Tara responds while keeping her eyes on her phone.

"Tara, you need to get a head start and that starts today. It's already June. Before you know it, the Fall semester will start," Samantha tells Tara as she prepares her plate.

"For the millionth time, Mom. I am not going to college. I have bigger things planned for my future. I can get into acting or something that college won't teach. Then I'm going to help others."

Samantha slams the breakfast plate in front of Tara. "I told you those are not real goals. You need an education to get ahead in life or you will end up like me, or worse. College is the only option for success."

"What, some whore that had a deadbeat cheating husband and got left for another woman? No thanks. I'll be smarter than that," Tara responds to her mom's scolding while texting on her phone again.

Samantha slams the pan of eggs on the stove. "You're such an ungrateful little bitch."

Tara finally looks up from her phone. "You wouldn't know a good man if he fell in your lap."

"And you do?" Samantha yells back at the top of her lungs. "I have worked two jobs to provide for you. Given you a decent life and you're going to throw it away on some stupid modeling dream."

Tara stands up and comes face to face with her mother. "I know myself. I believe in me if you want to or not. My dream is my dream. Why can't you just support my dreams?"

"You ungrateful bitch," Samantha yells as she slaps Tara across the face.

"No, not again." Tara fights back.

A scuffle between the two quickly dies after Samantha tosses Tara by her hair to the floor.

"I don't need you or your fucking college applications." Tara stands up, grabs her phone and runs out the door.

"You'll be back. You always come back," Samantha yells at Tara while fixing her hair. Samantha lights a cigarette and walks back into the kitchen.

Tara starts to walk as fast as she can in the hot summer sun. Hating her mother, her life, and the world.

A handsome, charming man pulls up to the curb in a nice truck.

"Hey, gorgeous, how are you?"

She blows him off and keeps walking.

The man continues to drive slowly next to Tara. "I'm going into town. I can drop you off wherever you're going. It's hot, and it's a long walk," the man tells her.

"It's bad for a model beauty like yourself to be walking in this heat in the middle of June. This summer heat can be dangerous."

"You think I'm a model?" Tara turns to him, smiling.

"Of course, I'm a talent scout and I know a natural

when I see one. You're a natural. Who do you model for?"

"No one right now. I'm sort of a free agent." "Well, jump right in. We can talk about you getting

some work on the ride to town."

Tara gets inside eagerly at the chance to hear her dreams potentially come true after a fight with her mother.

"Wow, nice ride for an old-school pickup truck." Tara tells the man as she rolls down her window.

"That's how I roll in the entertainment business. But I use this for hunting. This is a real classic here."

"What do you hunt?"

"Models. Beautiful ones like you."

Tara gives him an unpleasant look. She has heard those lame jokes before.

"I'm joking, of course. Deer mostly."

"I like fast cars like the ones in the movies." "Oh, this baby goes."

"Show me." Tara challenges the man.

The man rams the engine as hard as he can. The truck takes off, flying down the empty road ahead of them. The truck roars like an oncoming freight train.

Suddenly, out of nowhere, a deer runs from out of the bush and into the street.

The man swerves to avoid contact. He pitches the

truck to the right and almost rolls it. Its left tires lifting off the pavement and its right tires screeching and stuttering. The truck brutally slid sideways through the junction.

Tara screams thunderously out of thrill, excitement, and fear at the same time.

Her white shoes slam into the right-side view mirror as her feet hurl through the window, knocking the mirror in the middle of the street. The man takes his right arm and grabs Tara's elbow to pull her back in as he completes the left turn.

Tara sees a man in jogging clothes, his pale face stunned by the truck. The jogging man sees her white shoes hanging out the window.

The driver guns the truck's engine, and its tires screech and smoke as it speeds away ahead of the jogging man. The smell of rubber fills the streets as the wind blows through Tara's hair.

Tara looks down at her iPhone. It is 12:16. "Speaking of deer," she tells the man.

"That was close, but fun I guess. I'm Tara, by the way."

"John. John Dexter." "Nice to meet you, John."

"What brings you to White Pine?" John lights a cigarette.

"Home. I'm coming home."

John and Tara drive to Breitenbush and their journey has just gotten started. The start of the Lies Behind the Woods.

Sign-up For the next chapter

www.bradleycornish.com

https://www.facebook.com/AuthorBradleyCornish

Dark Obscurity

"Oh, Allison when will you learn your lesson?"

It may be Christmas break, but Allison can feel the heat.
Instead of studying for her finals, she was caught up having
sex with her no-good ex-boyfriend, Mark. He is selfish and a
non-apologetic serial cheater. The sex was good, but it leaves
her hollow afterward. Allison has a supportive family, and
she is looking forward to taking a break away from the
University of Columbia in New York and spending the
holidays with them back in Dakota.

A meek voice catches her attention before she leaves her
class, turning to a hot guy she dubbed as Mr. Tardy as he
either never turns up for class, or if he does, he is always
very late. He sheepishly introduces himself as Jack Corrode
and asks if she would like to go for a coffee. Over a caramel
macchiato, they make small talk, laughing about his 'chronic
tardiness' – until he gets a phone call that makes him edgy.

"I'm not going anywhere."

When Jack ends the call; his demeanor has changed. The
easy-going smile is cranked a little tight around his mouth,
and there is an edge in his eyes. Allison is disappointed when

he mentions that he needs to go, but quickly amends when he asks for her company back to his place.

"I sort of have a business that I run, and it pays pretty."

When they head to his super expensive car, Allison's jaw drops. Something in the back of her head tries to figure out how he could afford such a high-class vehicle when he is only a college student. She can't help but draw Jack up against Mark – and feels safe enough to slip into the car.

"I'm sort of a delivery boy. I pick expensive things up and deliver them."

They pull into an insanely luxurious mansion, stunning Allison once more. No one is around, so there's plenty of time for some hot and heavy petting. They've only known each other for one afternoon, but Jack literally rocks her world. It is a thrill she doesn't want to come down from.

Not long after – the phone rings and Jack hurries off downstairs and promises to bring back tea with round two. Stretching her muscles, Allison spreads back into the bathtub and awakes sometime later, after falling to a light doze. The place is in darkness and no one is around. Not even Jack.

"I am going to tell you this once; you should stay away from Jack Corrode. The only thing he attracts is trouble."

An ominous man startles her with this warning, but Allison is not just a pretty face. She is stubborn to boot and isn't the type of girl that stands and takes orders. Or threats. Jack hasn't just vanished into thin air; he's been taken somewhere.

Allison does whatever it takes, even going undercover to get answers. It leads her down the seedy road of a Mexican drug cartel, where violence, blood, and money go hand in hand – or hand around the throat.

Suddenly, there is a lot to break open about Jack behind the handsome face and good lay.

LIES BEHIND THE WOODS

BRADLEY CORNISH